THE
ANDROMEDA
FORCE

I0634901

By DAVID KANTORSKI

Copyright © 2023 by David Kantorski.
All rights reserved.

No part of this publication may be copied, reproduced in any format by any means, electronic or otherwise, without the prior consent from the copyright owner and publisher of this book. This is a work of fiction. All characters, names, places and events are the product of the author's imagination or used fictitiously. For information contact: contact@nanithedog.com

With deep gratitude and affection, I dedicate this book to my beloved parents, whose unwavering love and support have been my guiding light throughout life, and to my cherished friend, Evelyn Rosa, whose friendship has enriched my journey in countless ways.

Table of Contents

Chapter 1

"I still say this is a suicide mission/' Captain

Asterism stated as he sat in the cockpit of a

commandeered spaceship in the Bormino star

system, where a major battle raged.

"You knew the risks before agreeing to this

mission. If I recall, wasn't it you who said you

wanted to get away from your nagging wife and

children who demand your constant attention?"

Candar Mensa asked, smiling as she poked the

captain in the arm.

"You got me there. But I have the feeling something is going to go wrong with this operation."

"Something always goes wrong but we adjust and overcome the setbacks. Funny, you didn't complain about stealing this ship from one of Nova Spectrum's bases."

"Stealing a ship is easy, but what we are about to do is another matter."

"There is risk in every mission we undertake, so I suggest you put your big-boy pants on and start thinking positive for once. The Grand Oracle needs the data disks we have orders to steal."

"If I don't survive this mission, promise me you will make sure my wife has all the money she needs to live a good life. Also, tell my family I love them because if you don't, I will come back to haunt you."

"I can't do that since you won't die during this mission, and your family already knows how much you love them."

"Promise me you will do as I ask."

"I will see what I can do about your wishes."

"That's good enough for me. We are approaching the Mars Destroyer now."

Candar looked and saw one of Nova's battleships loom large in the view port window above a moon base.

"What are we risking our lives for this time?"

"Information the Grand Oracle needs so she can determine what events will unfold in the very near future," Candar responded.

"We always do the dirty work for others/' the captain stated.

"You like the adrenaline rush and cheating death."

"But this time around death is coming for me."

Candar fell silent. She wore a red uniform she had stolen for this mission so she could fit in. She looked like a twenty-year-old except for her hands, which were ancient-looking due to an evil curse that was slowly killing her. She never seemed to age. She had shoulder-length brown hair, peach-colored eyes, and the body of a beauty queen. She was most of the time optimistic but could be decisive and impulsive as well. Her eyes sparkled with hope.

Candar didn't have any military rake since she wasn't enlisted in any army. She had a reputation known throughout several galaxies for being a fierce defender of justice and peace. Her reputation had gained her both friends and enemies through the years. In the present, it seemed as though she had more enemies than friends. Often, Candar would travel with the high-ranking military officials or low-ranking soldiers; it didn't matter to her.

Candar and Captain Asterism had been on many missions in the past. They had seen their share of danger. They had also saved lives. The captain was the best pilot in the business with the exception of one other person. This other person was Orion Nebula. But she didn't know where

Orion was now, so she was stuck with her current pilot.

"We are being hailed."

"Give them this code and meet me in the cargo bay with the others," Candar said as she got up and left the cockpit.

"This is X9D4 reporting in," Captain Asterism stated.

"Mars Destroyer to X9D4, what is the password?"

"GTR5."

"You may approach. Go to landing spot 2000 and wait for a greeting party."

Captain Asterism guided the ship to the right location and landed. Before leaving the cockpit, he powered everything down.

Without saying a word, Candar pressed a button and the ship's hatch door opened. A greeting party stood at attention.

"I need to see your papers," the commanding officer of the group said.

Candar gave her papers to the officer.

"Everything is in order. You may go about your business. Enjoy your stay."

Candar turned to Captain Asterism only when the officer turned away. "You are to stay onboard. We may need to make a quick exit. Keep the engines running."

Without saying a word, Candar led her group of two hundred soldiers away from the ship and along the landscape of the Bormino Moon, where a moon base was located. She noticed her spies were spaced about the area as the group made their way closer to the base. Candar looked above as spaceships battled each other. She watched as a ship was hit and started falling to the ground around the area where she was now. Her groups made a dash for cover among military equipment littering the surface of the moon. The shrapnel from the ship came down with a loud bang. Fires started here and there. The smell of fuel showered the area and produced a thick black smoke.

It was with caution that Candar led the group through a minefield. One misstep and everyone would die. The moon base was still a ways to go as the battle above raged on. Candar closed her eyes and tried to concentrate on where to move next. She tapped into an ancient wisdom that only a few could tap into. It had taken her years to master her many talents but now she realized her past sacrifices were paying off in the present. She could do some amazing things. Candar also realized that because of her powers many feared her so much they wanted her dead.

Taking another step, she walked out of the minefield and waited for her team of soldiers to make it out as well. When the group was clear of the minefield, they waited for Candar to make a move. The ground all around them shook as spaceships continued to fall to the ground, which in turn started new fires and caused black columns of smoke to form. The smells of burning flesh and death were everywhere.

Candar led the group up a hill, her mind racing as she stopped walking, and she closed her eyes. With her mind, she searched the area for threats and found one nearby. She opened her eyes and took a few steps forward as a large creature appeared from behind a tree. The creature was as large as a bear with six sets of hands and sharp claws. It was covered in a thick fur, had green eyes and a large mouth with teeth resembling that of a shark. As the creature charged at Candar, she reached for her death wand, a plasma sword with multiple functions, taking it out of a sheath she wore around her waist. The death wand gave off a bright white light as she positioned herself in a combat stance. Candar waited patiently for the beast, who was three times her own height and several times her weight. The beast let out a loud roar as it sped forward. Candar was knocked to the ground. She waved to her troops not to attack and rose to her feet. The beast was fast and trying to slice her midsection open. She jumped back and pranced around, looking for the right moment to attack. All the beast's clawed hands came within inches of gutting her. Candar struck, slicing her death wand through the beast and cutting it in two pieces. Orange blood splattered the ground and the smell of blood hung in the air.

Candar knelt by the dead beast, feeling sorry she'd had to kill it. She didn't like killing creatures. It was evil people she would rather deal with, not creatures. Candar rose from the ground and continued to move forward, closer to the moon base. The soldiers with her kept silent and followed their leader.

Chapter 2

Candar Mensa walked to a door providing entry to the moon base. Security officers stood in front of the door with weapons drawn.

"Identify yourself/' a guard demanded.

Candar looked at the guard a moment. "You need to let us enter the base now."

The guard who had spoke, turned to the other guards. "We need to let them enter the base."

"This isn't proper protocol. Make them show us their papers/' a guard objected.

Candar stood silent, using the power of her mind to manipulate the guards. "Everything is in order. We must pass now without delay."

The head guard lowered his weapons and turned to the other guards. "Everything is in order. They must pass now without delay." He reached for the doorknob and opened the door to the base, allowing Candar and her soldiers to enter.

Candar and her soldiers entered a narrow hallway, but they didn't get far before a checkpoint appeared. She worried time was running out to complete her mission before Nova Spectrum arrived and shut her mission down.

An elderly woman stood behind a counter. "I need to see your papers please."

"My papers are in order; you don't need to see them. Let me pass," Candar stated.

"You may pass," the woman said as she pressed a button opening a door for them to walk down another hallway.

Candar walked down the hallway, knowing she was near the location her intelligence reports had stated the information she needed was stored. She came to a T intersection in the hallway and turned to the right. This hallway was long and seemed to go on forever. She came to a red door with soldiers guarding it.

A man stood behind a glass enclosure. Candar could sense this person had a strong will and knew her powers of persuasion wouldn't work on him. She handed the soldier her papers before he even asked for them. It seemed like a long time passed before he handed back the papers to Candar.

"You may enter but your soldiers must remain in the hallway."

Without saying a word, Candar walked toward the red door. As soon as it opened, she stepped inside. She took a few steps and stopped. Before her was a long hallway with lasers built into the walls and floor. They were being deactivated as she stood and watched. With the lasers deactivated, she walked down the hallway that had several offshoots and turned to the left. Guards stood by the entrance of a room filled with computer banks. The room had several levels, some with stairs and other with lift pads. It seemed to have no end.

Candar also noticed several guards positioned

about the room at every level. She walked a short

distance and stepped on a lift pad. Candar entered

the level she needed to go to and the lift pad

activated, moving up to level 95. Stepping off the

lift pad, she walked onto a metal platform filled

with computer banks. Knowing which computer

bank she needed, she walked over to it.

"Place your right hand in front of the

scanner," a computerized voice ordered.

Candar held her right hand in front of a

screen and a blue light scanned her hand.

"Step forward and place your left eye near the

scanner."

Candar saw a small eye scanner emerge from the computer bank. She stepped closer to it and a green light scanned her eye.

"Place your left hand on the scanner."

Candar saw a hand scanner move out of the computer bank. She placed her left hand on it and waited. A small needle came forward to take a blood sample, puncturing one of her fingers, then retreated.

"State your name."

"Commander Lunar Solstice," Candar replied as she touched a small device to change her voice.

"Your identity is confirmed. You may proceed to seek data cards."

Relieved, Candar entered a code to retrieve the first data disk the Grand Oracle needed. Lights flashed on the computer bank. A wave of cold air came from the computer as it erupted in sound. A small tray opened to reveal a small data disk in a protected case. Candar placed this disk in a waterproof pouch and then in a pocket on her uniform.

"Delete all references to the data on the file I just downloaded," Candar said.

The computer deleted the file from the computer. Then Candar entered a code for the next data disk she needed. It took a minute for the file to download and be pressed onto a data disk. As before, a door opened and Candar took the disk, placing it in a different waterproof bag then into her pocket. She told the computer to delete the file and it took a minute to delete.

There was only one more file she needed. She placed the code into the computer, but this time things went horribly wrong. An alarm sounded and lights on the computer were flashing red.

"You entered a wrong password. You do not have clearance to retrieve this file."

Candar kicked the computer, hoping the alarm would stop but it didn't and instead kept repeating the same message. She removed her death wand from its sheath and slashed at the computer. This split the computer in two. Data disks fell onto the metal walkway. She reached into the computer and grabbed the data disk she needed, placing it in another waterproof bag and then into her pocket. Candar took her death wand and managed to cut the computer into pieces. She kicked the destroyed computer and it fell to the next level below.

Guards swarmed around her, blocking her exit route. Plans were forming in her head as they advanced. She had been in worse situations than this before and always managed to find a way of escape.

"You're surrounded and have no chance of leaving. Place your weapon on the walkway. Resist and you will die. Hand over the data disks you stole," a chief guard ordered.

Candar said nothing as she was thinking about her escape. She was running out of options, but one plan coursing through her mind she knew would work. Taking her death wand, she sliced through the metal walkway just as the guards

25

around her opened fire with their blaster rifles. The metal walkway fell to the level below with a loud bang. Candar recovered quickly and as she stood up, she pressed a button on her death wand. She pulled out a blaster in her other hand and jumped off the metal walkway. Her plasma sword had multiple uses. As she hovered down to the first level, she fired her blaster at guards who turned their attention to her. She reached the first level and put her blaster away as she swung her death wand around, cutting through bodies as easily as a knife cutting through butter.

Alarms were deafening and the smell of blood hung in the air. Candar ran into a hallway and reached the area where lasers were built into the wall and ceiling. She had to pass this section and reconnect with her soldiers so they could leave the base. Candar reached into a pocket, took out a small golden ball the size of an orange, and tossed it upward. She called it a death ball. It moved forward, firing white laser beams at the laser minefield and started destroying it as guards attacked her at close range.

Candar kept one eye on those attacking her and another on the progress of her death ball. She stepped forward as the last set of lasers remained to be destroyed. The space filled with smoke and smelled like melted wires.

Candar reached the door and pressed a button, then stepped into a hallway and slashed the control panel, preventing the guards from getting to her. She was safe for the moment but wondered how long that would last. Candar had to get back to

her soldiers and leave this base at once.

Chapter 3

"Well, it's about time the sewer rat makes an appearance," Nova Spectrum stated with a smile as her soldiers laughed.

Candar still had her back to Nova, but she knew the voice well. It was the voice of evil. She turned and looked at Nova, who blocked her way forward, for a moment. Candar noticed Nova was wearing a red military uniform with black, latex, thigh-high, stiletto-heeled boots and long, over-the-elbow black gloves. She saw red horns running along Nova's arms and legs, a snake-like tongue, two massive blue horns protruding from her head, and bloodworms for hair. She gazed into the cold, coal-black eyes for a moment. They were devoid of joy, happiness, and mercy. All Candar saw in Nova's eyes was a deep anger and a smoldering hatred. Nova towered over Candar, standing close to seven feet tall. But Nova's height didn't scare her a bit. What scared Candar was the evil Nova represented to the worlds she visited. It was her charismatic way of seducing good people to do evil that Candar feared.

Nova took a step toward Candar. Her bloodworm hair moved about, stretching to try to bite Candar in the head and feast on her flesh.

Candar stood her ground and didn't flinch.

"Give me the data disks you stole from the base," Nova demanded with her hand stretched out in an open palm.

"And if I refuse, what happens then?"

Nova stepped aside so Candar could see the hallway with the dead bodies of her soldiers. "If you refuse to hand over the data disks, you will die like your soldiers littering the hallway. They will provide food for my hair for days, if not weeks, to come." Nova laughed along with the soldiers who stood behind her.

Sorrow and anger filled Candar and stirred her into action. She reached into her pocket and took out her death ball. It floated away from her and started firing white laser beams at the soldiers standing beside Nova.

"You can't defeat me. You're at a disadvantage. I have the upper hand in this situation/' Nova announced with an evil grin.

Candar said nothing and stood watching her death ball kill Nova's soldiers. It only took a few moments for the death ball to strike them down. Now the two of them stood alone in the hallway.

"It appears we are on equal footing and your advantage has been taken off the playing field."

The sound of soldiers running about and dying filled the hallway with sound. It was now that Nova took her own death ball out of her pocket, and it floated in the air near Candar. Her death ball was the size of an orange and as black as her eyes. It shot a red laser beam at Candar's feet.

"That was a warning shot. Hand over the data disks and join me or die. I won't make this offer again/' Nova threatened.

"You will pay for killing my soldiers."

"You are no match for me."

Candar pulled her death wand out of its sheath and rushed forward in a fighting stance, anger flowing throughout her body. She swung her plasma sword at Nova's midsection, but Nova produced her own death wand and both swords slashed into each other. Red and white sparks were moving around them. The smell of electricity filled the hall.

More of Nova's soldiers appeared with their weapons drawn ready to attack, then even more soldiers appeared. Candar wasn't worried at all. She had been in worse situations than this and always managed to survive. She had to work out a plan. Candar held out her hand and her death ball appeared. It shot laser beams at the lights in the hallway, plunging everyone into darkness as the death wands clashed and clashed again. The plasma swords gave off an eerie light and the sound of a low hum filled the hallway.

Candar motioned for her death ball to attack the soldiers and their cries of pain filled the space where she stood. Bodies littered the hallway and Candar had to be careful where she stepped. One wrong move and she would fall.

Nova moved forward while slashing her death wand. Candar defended herself as the swords clashed and clashed again. She was pushed up against a wall and dived to the floor in an effort to slash through one of Nova's legs. But Nova moved out of the way in time. Candar took the moment to stand up as Nova got into a fighting stance herself.

"You're growing tired. You won't last long," Nova threatened.

"The only thing I am growing tired of is your mouth," Candar replied as Nova's death ball fired a red laser beam at her and she deflected it with her sword.

Nova moved in closer and swung her sword, trying to get an advantage, when Candar, anticipating the move, brought her sword up to clash their swords together. They both fell after getting tangled up in dead bodies scattered about the floor. Nova rose first while Candar sheathed her sword to get a better position in the pitch-black hallway. The only light was Nova's plasma sword, which was glowing red.

Candar moved about silently while keeping her eyes on Nova. Taking her death wand out of its sheath, Candar sprang forward. She swung her death wand at Nova's face and came close to hitting her. Nova had to move away so quickly that she fell over the dead bodies littering the hallway. Candar stood over Nova with her death wand over her head. She brought the death wand down fast, but Nova brought her death wand up as the death wands clashed. Sparks were flying about and the smell of electricity filled the hallway. Intense light, both white and red, glowed as Nova rose from the floor. Nova attacked Candar with a few fast swings of the death wand. Candar stepped back under the pressure but was able to block the death blows from her opponent.

"Give up, sewer rat."

"Never!"

Candar swung her death wand around and attacked with renewed strength. She didn't know how long she could continue fighting due to the death curse that had been placed on her by an evil witch. The curse always put her in danger and made her tired, so much so she had to rest. She needed someone's protection when she was too tired to fight. But there was no one nearby to help her now. Candar had no choice but to keep fighting and she had her dead soldiers to inspire her.

"Give me the data disks now!"

"Are you growing impatient, Nova? That's not like you."

Candar stepped back as Nova exploded with powerful blows from her death wand. She fought as hard as she could manage in an effort to stay live. Then her death ball shot Nova, but she deflected it.

Candar moved to avoid Nova's death wand and hit a steam pipe. Nova stepped right under the severed pipe while hot steam blasted her in the face. She fell to the floor, screaming in pain. It was now Candar knew she had a way to escape. She ran down the corridor with her death wand, taking out the lights as her death ball fired white laser beams at enemy soldiers. The alarms going off gave

Candar a headache. She made her way to the door

that would lead to her safety.

Chapter 4

Candar opened the door and stepped outside. After shutting the door, she slashed the control panel so her enemies couldn't get to her. But when she turned around, there were soldiers with their weapons drawn, ready to shoot. Candar slammed her death wand onto the ground, which sent shockwaves strong enough to lift most of the soldiers off the ground and crashing into trees.

Those that remained fired their weapons as Candar's death ball moved about, killing soldier after soldier. Moving fast, she blocked the blaster fire with her death wand, started shooting her own blaster at the enemy, and ran. She was doing everything to make it harder for her enemy to target her.

Candar touched her ear. "Captain, I need evac now! Captain, are you there?"

A wave of worry passed through Candar. She hoped nothing was wrong with the ship and that the captain was still alive. She pressed a button on her death wand and rose into the air above the minefield while shooting her blaster. When her feet touched the ground again she tapped her com link. "Captain, are you there? Respond now!"

When no response came from the captain, worry seeped into her mind. Candar resorted to her backup plan, taking the matter in her own hands.

"Computer, engage in evacuation protocol one now," Candar ordered as she spoke into a small com link.

The ship came to life and flew into the air. It was at this moment that she remembered the captain's worry that the mission would end in failure. Candar's ship flew over to where she stood but it didn't land. The cargo bay door opened and Candar jumped into the ship. She pressed a button to close the door and another one to activate a force field around the ship.

While the ship flew about, wreaking havoc throughout the area around the moon base, her mind was on Captain Asterism. She could sense enemy soldiers onboard her ship. Candar reached into her flight suit and took out her death ball, allowing it to search the ship and attack the enemy soldiers who were waiting for her. Moving through the ship, she held her death wand, ready for an attack.

Two soldiers attacked. One soldier stood behind Candar while the other stood in front of her. She sliced through the soldier in front of her, killing him, then jumped to the floor while throwing her death wand into the chest of the soldier behind her. Before she could stand up, another soldier appeared, ready to attack. Candar opened her right hand, calling for her death wand to return to her. The death wand slammed into her hand as she rose from the floor and pierced the soldier in the heart before he had a chance to shoot. She could hear soldiers yelling as her death ball moved about the ship.

Candar walked down a narrow hallway as silently as she could. To her left was a closed door. She pressed a button, and it opened without any sound. Stepping into the kitchen, a blaster rifle went off, but Candar's death wand absorbed the blow. Laser grenades were thrown at her, but she sliced them in half while still trying to figure out where the enemy soldier was hiding. With her death wand, she slashed at the lights and the room fell into darkness. Candar crouched down behind a row of cabinets running below a stove. Her ears were focused on any sound that would give away the enemy, who was in the room with her.

Candar reached into her flight suit and took out a couple of flash grenades. She threw them in different directions. When they exploded, they produced a blinding light that lasted just long enough for Candar to spot her enemy. She stood and ran over to the woman who held a blaster in one hand and a laser dagger in the other. The enemy soldier fired her blaster and brought her laser dagger down hard, trying to slash Candar in the face. But Candar moved her death wand to deflect the blaster fire. Then she held her death wand near her face so both the laser dagger and her death wand collided.

The enemy soldier kicked Candar in the chest, causing her to fall to the floor on her back. Candar's death wand fell out of her hand and rolled around on the floor away from her. The soldier's knees slammed into Candar's chest, momentarily knocking the air out of her lungs. Candar turned to look at her death wand and saw someone pick it up. Meanwhile, the soldier on top of Candar raised her hands, holding the laser dagger, ready to plunge it into Candar's head. Candar opened her right hand and concentrated on her death wand. It pulled away from the soldier holding it and entered her hand. She brought it up and stabbed the soldier with the dagger in the heart. Then she pushed the dead soldier off her body and stood up. The other soldier in the room fired his blaster but Candar was ready. The blaster fire bounced about the room, deflected by her death wand.

Then a soldier jumped down from a trap door in the ceiling and landed on Candar, knocking her to the ground. He wrapped his arms around her neck and started to choke her as the other soldier in the room came out of hiding with his blaster drawn. Just as the soldier with the drawn blaster fired, the ship moved hard to the right. This gave Candar the moment she needed. She moved her wrists just enough so that her death wand, still in her hands, could slice the soldier's head off. The blaster fire hit the dead soldier as he fell to the floor. The soldier died so quickly he didn't have time to scream.

Now Candar focused her attention on the soldier before her. He was twice her height and three or four times her weight, yet she didn't have the slightest fear running through her mind.

"They will make me a god after I kill you," the soldier announced.

Candar swung her death wand around to deflect the blaster fire from the soldier's gun. But then she decided she had to do more. She had to bring the fight to the soldier and be in charge. The soldier fired his blaster as the ship shifted to the left. Candar moved with the ship and sliced the blaster in half.

"You still think you can kill me?" Candar asked.

The soldier threw his broken blaster on the floor and reached behind him to grab two handfuls of knives. He threw the knives at Candar, and one by one she cut them in half with her death wand. But two laser daggers hit her, one in the right leg and the other in the left leg. She went down, screaming in pain, as the soldier rushed to move in and finish her off. The ship pulled up with out warning so quickly the soldier fell to the floor. When he stood up, Candar's death ball entered the room and fired white laser beams at the soldier, killing him. She heard a loud thud as he fell to the floor, lifeless.

Candar pulled out one of the laser daggers and then the other one. She closed her eyes as intense pain and blood swirled around in the air. She had a strong feeling that all the enemy soldiers on the ship were dead. She tried to get up but couldn't. On the verge of passing out, Candar closed her eyes and tried to calm herself and push the pain aside. It took time, but she managed to stand and leave the room. She put her death ball back in her flight suit. Then she put away her death wand. She stepped over the bodies littering the hallway while hugging the blood-splattered wall. She saw the cockpit door was open slightly and then she entered the room. It took her a moment, but she found the captain on the floor in a pile of his green blood. His body was covered with the scaly skin of a snake. His keyhole-shaped eyes still had life in them. His body had no hair. His mouth was filled with sharp teeth.

In shock, Candar fell to the floor and knelt beside the captain.

"Keep your promise to me," Asterism said as he died in her arms.

Bitter tears fell from her eyes as her dear friend left forever. Candar walked over to the pilot seat and pressed a button. A door opened in the command chair and out came two small universal healers. She placed one on her right leg and another on her left leg, and the healers started healing her body. She flew away from the moon base moments before it exploded. Then she joined the raging battle around a space station and started attacking enemy ships.

Chapter 5

Hatred burned in her heart as Nova Spectrum

sat in her fighter ship taking out targets she wanted

destroyed in the Bormino system. Plans were being

followed and she was alert to the threat of her rival,

Candar Mensa. She blew up a ship next to her and

regarded it as practice while looking for her rival.

As Nova sat in the cockpit, her thoughts drifted to

Trifid Hedin, one of the greatest wizards to have

lived. It was Nova's greatest ambition to bring him

back to life. Most people regarded him as evil, but not Nova.

Her target was enemy forces, or those who supported the Grand Oracle. She was an expert at flying spaceships, but she enjoyed flying her fighter most of all.

Nova desired power, and her plan to bring back to life a dead wizard was just the beginning. There was much she had to do before she could attempt to bring the wizard back from the dead. She would let nothing stand in her way. In the view port of the cockpit she saw several enemy ships. She decided to follow one of them. The ship she was tracking was about to attack one of her battleships. She waited for the right moment when that ship entered her gun sights. Then she fired and watched as the ship she attacked broke apart in front of her eyes. A dark smile fell across her face.

Her enemies were like angry bees and there were too many to count. But it was easy to kill bees and she knew how to squash them. Nova wished it was more challenging to kill her enemies. Taking down a worthy opponent always proved more fun to her.

This was the first military campaign of a war she wanted to start. This battle around the Bormino system would provide the chance to assess her fighting force and help her determine who she should move up the ranks as leaders.

Nova spotted a cluster of enemy fighters straight ahead and fired her weapons, destroying three fighters. Her eyes darted about, scanning for her next target, when alarms went off in the cockpit. Nova then spotted Candar Mensa's ship. Nova opened fire but other ships were in the way. She was in hot pursuit of Candar's ship when one of her fighters pulled up in front of her as she was ready to shoot at Candar's ship. Nova cursed under her breath as her eyes were pinned to Candar's ship. Nova could only watch as Candar destroyed ship after ship with ease.

All the ships fighting the Grand Oracle's forces belonged to Nova. The damage Candar was inflicting on her fighting force was taking a toll. Nova blew up one of her own fighters to have a clear shot at Candar's ship. Nova fired, but Candar managed to avoid the weapon's fire. Nova fired again, only to feel disappointment once again. When Nova was about to strike again, fighter ships got in the way of her plans. Nova had to fly around them. Then the third time Nova attacked, she almost hit Candar's ship. But instead, she hit one of the big cruisers as it got in the way of her pursuit of Candar. Anger filled her heart. The loss of the ship she'd just destroyed weighed heavy on her heart. She knew everyone on the ship and was amazed at their dedication to her. But now they were all gone. She wanted Candar to pay with her life.

Nova lost track of Candar's ship then spotted it again flying between two massive battle cruisers. Following Candar's ship, Nova fired her weapons as the gap between the battle cruisers became smaller and smaller. Nova's weapon fire hit both battle cruisers and missed Candar's ship. Anger engulfed her. She hoped she would make it through the gap, as the two battle cruisers were pulling away from each other.

Nova passed the two large battle cruisers and saw Candar's ship in front of her. She didn't hesitate to attack. This damaged the shield protecting Candar's ship. Attacking again, Nova watched as repeated explosions erupted, much to her delight. Then she saw Candar's ship head for the surface of the planet below. It was zigzagging out of control with a plume of smoke trailing behind. The ship then sped toward the upper atmosphere of the planet below.

Assuming Candar Mensa would die soon, Nova returned to the raging space battle. She took out a few more enemy fighters before deciding she should return to her ship.

Power and the desire for control entered her mind as Nova arrived back on her flagship. She stepped out of her fighter and walked out of the cargo bay. She could almost feel the presence of Trifid Hedin's spirit as she walked swiftly to an elevator that led to the bridge. Once she got off the elevator, it was a short distance to the bridge. She reached the blast doors and a door opened to the bridge. She noticed that the command center was alive with activity. Nova walked over to take a seat near the captain in the center of the room. Her bloodworm hair swirled about. Her coal-black eyes noticed everything going on in the room. She was impressed with what she saw.

"Reports! Where are my reports?" Nova demanded, holding out her right hand to receive a data tablet.

She looked over the reports quickly and noticed that everything seemed to be going as planned. It took but a moment to analyze them.

"Open a com link."

"Ready."

"This is Nova Spectrum and I have good news. Candar Mensa is dead. I enjoyed killing her; she was such a roadblock to my plans. I hope you are as happy as I am to know of her demise. I also wanted to tell you I demand the immediate arrest of the Grand Oracle. This isn't all. I want the oracles of light to work for me. Any oracles that refuse my offer will die. You have one hour to make your decision. If the Grand Oracle isn't arrested and turned over to me, all will die."

Taking her seat in the cockpit of the ship, she pressed a button on the side of the armrest. "Prepare my fighter for a trip to the surface. You must alert my students to meet me on the surface as well. I want my ship ready in ten minutes."

With her treat exposed, Nova knew the Grand Oracle wouldn't give up the fight. She also knew the soldiers on the ground would defend the Grand Oracle with their lives. *Fools,* she thought. They were no match for her and because of her powers, she knew they would try to stop her. *Let them try; it will all be for nothing.*

"I want a squadron to search for Candar's ship. When you find it, bring me her body," Nova commanded as she turned to the captain.

"As you wish, Nova," the captain replied as he sent the orders down the chain of command.

Nova was one step closer to reaching her goals now with Candar dead. The Grand Oracle would be next. But in the Grand Oracle's case, she didn't intend to kill her. She would use the Grand Oracle by extracting information out of her. She could always kill her later and it was subject to change. If, for instance, the Grand Oracle fed her lies and no accurate information, then she would kill her. Nova believed she was in control of the situation and with one foe dead, all she had to do was capture the Grand Oracle alive. In fact, one of her spies was already on the ground carrying out

her plans now. She could almost taste victory. But

then again, an all-consuming burning hate filled her

when she thought of Candar. She wanted her body

so she could desecrate it in public for every star

system to see. This would help put fear into the

minds and hearts of her enemies.

Chapter 6

The Grand Oracle wasn't fazed at all by Nova

Spectrum's threat to arrest her. She'd had to deal

with threats her whole life. Ever since she was a

young child, she knew she was different from

everyone else. At an early age, she was separated

from her parents because she had a special gift.

When she was four years old, she started having

visions. When her visions came true most of the

time, there were people who feared her. A small

group looked at her visions as a positive benefit.

But this was a small group, while most shunned her

when she was a girl. Many more wanted her

removed from the community. They thought she

was a freak with a weird power. They didn't trust

her visions.

The Grand Oracle's visions were not always

accurate. This is why she had to leave her parents to

develop her powers. It took dedication, practice,

and time but she was able to concentrate on the

correct vision each time she had one.

Now in the present she had perfected her

visions to such a point she was the leader of oracles.

It was her task or burden to train young girls so

they could help communities with their visions

throughout the vastness of space.

The Grand Oracle rose from a seat in the command center of a vast, ancient castle and turned to her second in command. "Lysithea, I will be in my meditation room. I don't want to be disturbed."

"I understand. I will place guards outside of the door so no one enters."

"Thank you, Lysithea."

The Grand Oracle walked to a massive blast door that could withstand a nuclear attack and waited for it to open. She had the appearance of a young woman of twenty, with long, curly, dark brown hair and stood five feet six inches tall. She had a third eye in the center of her forehead that was diamond-shaped. This eye was larger than her other two eyes. Her eyes were white when she was meditating and orange-colored when she was not meditating. She liked to wear a black flight suit with a black, hooded cape.

Once the blast doors opened, she walked across a hall to a room with a heavy door. She walked into the center of the room and sat down on a cushion with back support. The room itself was wide with a tall ceiling and smelled of pinewood. It was pitch-black, so much so that she couldn't see her hands. The Grand Oracle crossed her legs, closed her eyes, and started focusing on her breathing. She took in a long, deep breath and let it out slowly. Doing this repeatedly for several minutes took her to a point she wanted to reach. Now she was on the verge of falling into a trance-like state. Mystical vapors rose from small holes in the floor to aid her in reaching a trance.

She closed her eyes while focusing on the

raging battles. Almost at once, images appeared

and sounds filled the empty room. The Grand

Oracle opened her eyes. She saw several images

appearing before her. They looked like each was

projected onto its own screen. Moving her hands,

she pushed some images aside to focus on the

images she thought were most important.

Destruction and death were what the Grand

Oracle saw as she sat in her meditation room on planet

Bormino. She knew time was short. She could see the

battles going on all around the space station and the

damage it was doing. Time was short. There were

battles taking place in the air and under the sea.

Spaceships buzzed by with lightning speed. Some

crashed to the ground while others blew up in the sky,

raining down on the troops below. Soldiers on the ground were running here and there. They were attacking and being attacked as they fought for their lives.

The Grand Oracle closed her eyes once again as smoke rose in the room. She breathed in mystical vapors to sharpen her vision and help put her into a deeper trance-like state. She moved her hand and then opened her eyes to focus on a single ship.

Her eyes were drawn to a fighter, which was flying to the surface of the planet at too fast a rate of speed. She knew it was Candar Mensa's ship. A trail of smoke followed her ship and the ship itself was zigzagging out of control.

She could see Candar Mensa dressed in a blue flight suit and a black cloak, sitting in the cockpit of a spaceship. Candar's eyes sparkled with hope even though the Grand Oracle knew Candar was worried about her situation. She needed Candar to fight for her. The Grand Oracle was aware of an ancient death curse that was slowly killing Candar. She was still trying to find a cure or way to undo the curse but as of late still came up empty.

"This is the Light Bearer. I'm going down ... lost navigation ... can't eject..." the Grand Oracle heard Candar say.

The space station frantically tried to reach Candar. Now the Grand Oracle could see a massive trail of smoke trail the ship. She heard an explosion so powerful it moved her soul, making her shudder violently. Then it happened. Candar's ship crashed into the ocean.

The Grand Oracle had seen enough. She wondered if Candar was still alive. She didn't sense that she was dead. All she had was hope that Candar was still alive.

She rose from the floor as the images vanished, leaving the room totally dark, and walked to a door that opened. Bright light filled the room from a hallway as she stepped out of the room end entered the command center.

Survival of the oracles was on the Grand Oracle's mind as she stood in her command center. Both caution and safety prompted her to call Lysithea over to her.

"Lysithea, I need you to gather all the oracles and get them loaded onto the escape pods for evacuation. I need this done now. When you finish, send a message to Orion Nebula's nearest base

telling them we need Orion's help."

"I will do as you wish, Grand Oracle," Lysithea

replied with a short bow.

Lysithea Candela was in her early twenties

with a slim body and muscular arms and legs. She

had shoulder-length, lemon-colored, wavy hair, one

ear that was blue and another that was bright

yellow. She had four eyes, which were five-point-

star-shaped eyes that were dark teal-colored. She

had dark purple skin.

Lysithea left the command center and pressed an

alarm once out in the hallway.

The palace was filled with the sound of thousands of running feet. In a short amount of time, all the oracles stood at attention. Without saying a word, Lysithea led the mass mob down a flight of stairs. She led them down several more before leading them into a cargo bay area. In calm movements, all the oracles stood in front of four ships. Lysithea broke them down into different groups. When all the oracles were in the right group, Lysithea ordered them to enter the ships waiting to take them to safety.

With the first task done, Lysithea left the oracles and walked up several flights of stairs until she reached the communications room. She knew what she was ordered to do. She walked up to security officers. They allowed her to enter further into the communications room. Lysithea walked over to an

open communications terminal. She sent a coded

message to one of Orion's distant secret bases. Once

she was done, she left the room and reentered the

command center. She then took her place at a station

near the Grand Oracle.

Chapter 7

A massive battle was taking place just outside
the command center. Loud explosions and screams
of soldiers dying were heard from inside the
command center. Greed, power, and dislike for the
Grand Oracle rose to the surface of her heart. Lysithea
Candela, in the Grand Oracle's command center, did
not blink when she turned her stun gun toward the
Grand Oracle and shot her in the back. The Grand
Oracle fell to the floor with a loud thud.

Lysithea then turned her attention to the stunned security forces. She took out a couple before they fired back, sending the command center into a major firefight. Small fires erupted here and there. Lysithea threw grenades across the room and crawled on the floor to get a better vantage point.

Some security forces were moving about the room trying to get behind and surround Lysithea. She shot them as they moved, and they fell to the floor dead.

Sonic grenades were thrown nearby, where Lysithea was crouched behind a desk. She was able to put earmuffs on before the grenade went off. It produced an ear-splitting sound with powerful shock waves designed to burst a persons éardrums without ear protection. Due to the shock wave, she was pushed into the open.

Lysithea was grazed in the right arm by a blaster rifle before she had a chance to move to a safer position. Her only thought was she hoped she could hold out long enough until Nova arrived. She moved to a safer position, but the fight continued. Not satisfied, she moved around to avoid a situation were she was pinned down. For a while there was a stalemate. She didn't have an advantage over the security force in the room. They likewise didn't have the advantage over her.

Lysithea ejected a battery cartridge from her blaster and replaced it with a new one with a full charge on it. Then she continued to battle the security forces in the room as louder explosions erupted outside the command center.

A barrage of laser blaster fire hit the desk she was hiding behind, blowing it to pieces and starting a fire near her. She had no choice but to move. Crouching as near to the floor as she could, she moved into an open area when grenades hit the floor. Before they could go off, she moved behind a high bench. The grenades left a crater in the floor, sent shrapnel around, and produced a loud sound. Some of the shrapnel hit Lysithea in the left leg.

Now with Lysithea wounded, it gave the security forces the chance to position themselves around her. All they had to do now was to wait a little while before they moved in closer to capture or kill Lysithea. But they couldn't wait for long.

The lights in the room flickered for the first time as the battle outside the command center intensified. Canisters of knockout gas landed by Lysithea, who was forced to move from her position, and once again she was out in the open. A barrage of laser blaster rifles erupted near her. She was sure she was going to die when a massive sound shook the room. The blast doors to the command center were blown off their hinges and the doors slid on the floor and stopped in the middle of the room.

Nova stepped into the room and noticed the security forces that were still alive. A fierce battle was still raging in the room. She held out her hands over her head and focused her energy on the few fighting Lysithea. The weapons of the Grand Oracle's security force tumbled to the ground. Then the security team was thrown hard against the wall, dying a quick death. A sickening snapping sound was heard as bones were broken. When Nova lowered her arms, the security force fell to the floor dead. Silence fell upon the room. Then a rush of feet stamping on the floor filled the room as Nova's forces entered.

Joy came across Nova's face as she walked into the Grand Oracle's command center. She saw the Grand Oracle lying on the floor, motionless. Nova knew now with the capture of the Grand Oracle that she was in control. At a snail's pace, Nova walked to the Grand Oracle's chair and sat down. Once Nova was seated, she laughed, filling the room with a chill.

Lysithea approached Nova with a smile as she rose from the floor and then fell.

"Help her get up and bring her to me," Nova ordered.

Two soldiers help Lysithea stand and slowly walk over to Nova. When Lysithea was standing before Nova, she moved her hands over the wound on Lysithea's body. Almost at once the wounds healed. Then, restored, Lysithea knelt down before Nova.

"You have served me well and you will be rewarded," Nova said.

"We must kill the oracles that are waiting for evacuation," Lysithea replied.

"We will deal with them soon enough. First we must offer them a chance to join us."

"Is it true? Is the witch Candar Mensa dead?"

"Her fighter was badly damaged, out of control, and crashed on the planet. Her body hasn't been found yet, but I believe she is dead."

"This is good news for us," Lysithea announced.

"It is a time for celebration," Nova agreed.

"Now what are your plans?" Lysithea asked.

"Secure the Grand Oracle on a hover board and make sure you put stun cuffs on her wrists and ankles. I don't want her escaping. Make sure no one harms or kills her. I need to extract information from her."

A hover board the size of a cot floated into the room. Nova watched as the Grand Oracle was bound and secured. Soldiers surrounded the Grand Oracle as the hover board floated out of the room.

Now just Nova and Lysithea were the only ones in the room.

"What are my plans? Well, they are to bring back to life Trifid Hedin. But there are things we have to do before that can happen."

"How can I help you achieve your goal?"

"You will train oracles here in this castle. The oracles will work for us. We will need them to search for the Book of the Dead. Once we have this book, we can bring our wizard back to life."

"Where is the book now?"

"This is what you will have to figure out with the oracles you will train. The oracles of light movement are over. The oracles of dark are all yours to control."

"Where will you get these oracles for me to train?"

"We will take them from planets scattered throughout the galaxy. They will serve you or die. The choice will be theirs to make."

"What will you do with the Grand Oracle?"

"I will interrogate her and extract as much information from her as I can."

"What if she gives you false information?"

"In that event I will kill her."

"What will you do with Orion Nebula?"

"I will capture him and kill him, along with his meddlesome friends."

"The Andromeda Force must be destroyed as well."

"I agree with you, Lysithea. It will happen but it will take time to achieve our goals."

Chapter 8

Candar Mensa woke up. She had passed out
when her ship crashed into the ocean. She had a bad
headache, but otherwise she was fine. Candar was a
little disoriented. She closed her eyes and
concentrated on the task at hand. Wanting to get
out of the ship, she realized she wouldn't be able to
do it on the bottom of the ocean. Candar closed her
eyes and concentrated on lifting the ship off the sea
floor. Little by little the ship moved upward. When

the ship reached the surface, Candar opened her eyes. She didn't know how long it would stay floating in the water before it sank again. Candar walked out of the cockpit and over to the cargo bay door. She pressed a button to open the door and looked outside at a calm sea. Her eyes were drawn to the spaceships battling each other in the sky and in the ocean. She looked at the shore and knew the Grand Oracle's castle was nearby. She calculated the shore was about two or three feet away.

"Why is it nothing is ever easy?" she asked herself.

Candar closed her eyes a moment to prepare for what she had to do. Then with her eyes open, she stepped out of the ship and started running on top of the ocean water all the way to the shore. Now on dry land, she crouched down just outside the castle's cargo bay. She took a moment to take in the situation unfolding before her. From where she was she could see Nova Spectrum, her three students, several soldiers, and Lysithea Candella. There were also several large ships. Candar focused her attention on Nova's three students. She looked at Yospher Ejecta first. She had the face of a horse, body of a young woman, large, orange-cyan-colored eyes, short, blanched almond hair, a mouth of razor-sharp teeth, and a small, muscular, very attractive build.

Next, she looked at Denog Serpens. Candar was drawn to his left hand. It was nothing more than a burning, blood-red flame in the shape of a hand. Then she took in his large build and silver eyes. He had long, violet-colored hair and green, pointy ears.

Candar focused her attention on Nova's last student. She looked at Grifwid Gravity. Her eyes were drawn to his bright-orange-colored skin, peach-puff-colored hair, rosy-brown-colored eyes, and a tall, large, muscle-bound body.

Candar ran into the cargo bay of the castle, soaking wet from the crash landing in the ocean, and hid behind a row of boxes that were scattered about the room. From where Candar stood, she saw Nova, her students, and Lysithea Candela engaged in battle with the Grand Oracle's palace guards. Justice was on Candar's mind, as well as the survival of the oracles. She knew she had to stop Nova Spectrum's agenda, even if the price was her own life.

Candar stood in the docking bay of the palace waiting for the right moment to fight.

Nova Spectrum appeared to be winning the battle in the room, along with her students and Lysithea Candela.

Taking a chance, Candar took out her death wand, activated it, and came out of hiding to attack first. Her death ball hit Nova and knocked her over. She cried out in pain, then threw her own death ball into action as she rose from the floor with the quickness of an angry black panther, her death wand activated.

"Don't interfere. Leave Candar to me. Now kill them. Kill them all," Nova Spectrum ordered as she pushed Candar back, slashing at her wildly.

At this point, Candar took out her laser dagger, a small steel knife with a built-in laser in place of a sharp-edged, steel-pointed blade. In one hand she held the laser dagger while in the other was her death wand, a plasma sword with multiple uses. Nova held her death wand tightly in her hands and fought back.

"You will never best me, sewer rat. You're not even in the same league as me. Join me or die. Those are the only two choices you have."

"Never!" Candar yelled with renewed strength as she pushed Nova back.

"Then death is what you will get!" Nova shouted back as she pushed Candar into the center of the room. Most of the fighting stopped because no one loyal to Nova wanted to hit her with blaster fire. The same was true for Candar. The battle

intensified when Candar knelt on the floor for a

moment, eyeing crates piled high above her head.

Nova moved in, holding her death wand high over

her head, ready to strike a fatal blow. But at this

moment, Candar's death ball was about to strike

Nova with a white laser beam. While Nova moved

to block the blow from the death ball, Candar

sprang forward, stabbing Nova in the right leg. She

then jumped on top of the pile of crates she'd been

eyeing earlier. It all happened in a split second.

Candar could hear Nova screaming in pain like a

wounded animal. Nova jumped up on top of a pile

of crates near Candar and the battle continued.

Candar kept one eye out for Nova's death ball while

the other focused on her opponent.

Sweat poured down Candar's face as she clashed with Nova's death wand and had to turn around and block a red laser beam from Nova's death ball. Then Nova jumped onto the same crate Candar was standing on. The battle intensified as the death balls started moving faster and faster around the two of them. Nova swung her death wand at Candar, but she was ready and blocked the blow. Nova swung again and Candar jumped to the floor and sliced through several crates. Nova fell to the floor but made a quick recovery as she rushed at Candar, who blocked a killing blow with her own death wand. There seemed to be no end to the battle. But Candar was getting tired, and this would be a problem if the attack didn't end soon.

Nova attacked and Candar jumped to the floor as her death wand slipped out of her hands. Still on the floor, she retrieved her death wand and blocked Nova's death ball, then rose and clashed with Nova. Their death wands clashed continuously as Candar and Nova moved across the vast floor of the room. At this point, the fighting in the room stopped, as all eyes were glued to Candar and Nova engaged in a death duel.

Candar was growing tired and was afraid that she couldn't fight much longer. She pushed Nova forward but then Nova pushed her back several steps. Nova fought hard as Candar tried to keep the duel going. She wanted to find an opportunity or moment where she could strike her opponent and end the fight. Sweat was running down her face as she focused her attention on Nova's death ball and death wand. The plasma swords clashed, then Nova pushed Candar back near the entrance of the cargo bay. Nova ran forward and their death wands clashed again. Now they were standing on a dock right outside of the cargo bay. Nova lunged forward, causing Candar to move back into the cargo bay. It was now that Nova made her move. Nova used her powers and pushed Candar through a concrete wall. Candar hovered above the ocean as a concrete slab hovered nearby. Then Candar fell into the ocean and the concrete slab fell on top of her.

The battle in the room resumed as if nothing had happened, but both sides were motivated to fight to the death.

Chapter 9

Europa Comet was in charge of getting the

Oracles of Light to safety. These were the oracles

that the Grand Oracle wanted protected. In fact, the

Grand Oracle had told Europa on many occasions

that the Oracles of Light would play a significant

roll in future wars. It was the Grand Oracle's belief,

Europa recalled now, that the Oracles of Light

would push the balance of power to the side of

justice. Europa had been approached by the Grand

Oracle and given special tasks. One of these tasks was to learn how to pilot all kinds of spaceships. As the Grand Oracle put it, one day her piloting skills would be needed to save the oracles. Today was this day.

Europa wore a black flight suit as she sat in the captain's seat of the ship's command center. She was a young woman with blue hair and cranberry-colored eyes that sparkled in the sunlight. She was six feet tall with a well-toned body. She always had her favorite weapons with her, like laser knuckles, a laser rifle, and a plasma dagger.

"Activate the shields around our ships," Europa commanded.

"Shields are up."

"How are we with moving the oracles into ships one and two?"

"We are about halfway done with the transfer."

"That's not good enough. I'm leaving the command center to assist the oracles, but before I go, engage weapons and fire on our enemies. I will stay in touch with the command center through a com link, so keep me updated."

"Captain, leaving the command center," one of the crewmembers stated.

The doors to the command center opened and Europa stepped into a hallway and passed two guards protecting the command center. She touched her laser rifle attached to a belt around her hip, hoping she wouldn't need to use it.

There was chaos in a long hallway. She could hear shouting and felt the collective fear of the oracles around her. One of the oracles fell and Europa was there to help the young girl to her feet.

Europa pointed to three women. "You three come with me."

The four ran down to the end of ships one and two. When they reached the beginning of the third ship, Europa turned to two of the women. "Stay here and make sure the oracles are in two lines. The row to the right is to go to ship one and the row to the left must go to ship two."

Europa then ran down to the beginning of ship four with the last oracle with her. "Make sure the oracles leave this ship in two lines."

Europa then moved into the command center
of the fourth ship. She was alone when she received
a message.

" Captain, the force field around ships three
and four won't hold for much longer."

"How are we with evacuating the oracles
from ships three and four?"

"We are almost done, with just ten percent left
to move."

"I will be with you shortly. Set a hyperspace
jump for Orion Nebula's nearest base."

Europa walked over to the command chair,
sat down, pressed a few buttons, and entered a
code. Once the code was entered, she got up and
left the ship with the ship's self-destruct program

activated. She ran into the third ship and activated the self-destruct program on it.

When Europa left the third ship and entered the second ship, she detached the ships.

"All oracles are now in ships one and two."

"Good. I'm on my way."

Europa ran down a long hallway while oracles were moving about to claim their seats before the ships took off. It took a few minutes for Europa to reach the door just outside the ship's command center. Just when she was about to enter, the guards standing by the door opened fire on her. Europa jumped to the floor unharmed. She reached for her laser rifle and fired, missing both guards as she stood up. Before the guards could fire their weapons, Europa fired at the lights in the hallway, sending the hallway into total darkness.

Standing with her back against a wall, she stood with one hand on her rifle and her plasma dagger in the other hand. She strained her ears for any of the guards' movements and breathing. A long pause passed, then both guards attacked, firing their blasters and revealing their positions. Europa was hit in the leg and fell as she fired her blaster in the direction of one guard. She was rewarded by hearing the guard fall to the floor. The other guard knocked the rifle out of her hands, and it made a loud sound as it slid across the floor. She rolled around on the floor as silently as she could and took her plasma dagger out of a sheath, then activated her laser knuckles. The laser knuckles she wore on each hand looked like brass knuckles but had lasers built into them.

Europa rose from the floor and kicked where she thought the guard was standing and heard a gun fall to the floor. So now it would come down to a knife fight, and she was ready. Europa felt a whish of air as a laser dagger came close to hitting her. She moved back and out of the way just in time.

Her opponent's laser dagger gave off a red glow, while Europa's plasma dagger gave off a bright blue light. Europa moved to the left as her opponent's plasma dagger punctured the wall where her head had been moments ago. Then before Europa could move, she felt the weight of her opponent's body come crashing down on her wounded leg. Europa let out a cry of pain as her

enemy was trying to retrieve her plasma dagger.

Without any options left, Europa turned on her

laser knuckles and slashed her enemy's midsection,

killing her. Europa turned off her laser knuckles

and rested for a moment as footsteps came closer to

her.

"Captain, are you alright? Can you walk?" a

guard asked, shining a light on her.

"I could use some help getting up."

A few guards helped her to her feet and

helped her into the command center of ship one.

Once she sat down in her chair, she turned to the

guards. "I want you to stand guard outside the

command center. Identify the enemy. There might

be more onboard, so keep a watchful eye out for

anyone you think is a threat. Go now and don't let anyone enter the command center. Ships three and four are set to self-destruct at any moment now."

Without saying a word, the guards left and the doors to the command center were sealed shut. The bodies of the two enemies were dragged away so an investigation could begin.

"I need a universal healer for my leg."

A crewmember brought a brace forward, placing it on the captain's wounded leg. It had several lights, needles, and lasers that could heal almost anything. Once the universal healer was turned on, the lights lit up, needles punctured her skin, and healing lasers sprang into life.

"Is the course set for Orion Nebula's nearest base?"

"Yes, captain, and engines are fired up."

"How much time is left before ships three and four self-destruct?"

"Twenty seconds."

"Take us out of here now."

The ship rose from the floor, along with ship two, which was attached to ship one. Weapons were fired at a concrete wall to give the ship enough room to leave. Both ships left the castle and flew high into the atmosphere. When the ship reached space, it entered into a hyperspace jump but not before the captain and crew witnessed the space station explode.

The great loss of life and infrastructure hit Europa hard. She had several friends placed about the space station and moon base. Now they were just a memory. It was at this time she thanked the Grand Oracle for training her to pilot spaceships.

Now was not a time for sorrow. Now was the time for action. Europa had a tall task to perform and that was to save the oracles. She was committed to the task and was willing to sacrifice her life if it came to it so the oracles could live.

Chapter 10

A massive explosion ripped through the room in the oracle castle cargo bay as the ships Europa set to self-destruct went off. Several soldiers lay dead on the floor while others were moaning in pain.

Nova Spectrum rose to her feet and touched her com link. *"I* need a transport ship sent to my location now, and make sure you track the oracle ships that just left the planet."

Looking around the room, Nova felt a strong anger pass through her. She hoped Candar Mensa was dead now, but looking at the wreckage in the room and the vast number of dead littering the floor, she wished she could kill Candar again.

Turning to Lysithea, Nova said, "You will remain here to train the Oracles of the Dark. I also want you to put down this rebellion."

A ship arrived and Nova, along with her students, ran inside. In a moment, it was gone from sight. The shuttle reached Nova's main battle cruiser, entering a huge cargo bay. Once the ship landed, Nova wasted no time and emerged from the shuttle to quickly make her way to the cockpit.

Death was what Nova Spectrum wanted for the oracles she was pursuing as she sat in the cockpit of her battle cruiser. She knew as long as they were alive, they were a threat and she needed to silence them with death.

"Fire again. I don't want them to reach Orion's hidden base."

"They can't hold out for much longer," one of Nova Spectrum's officers replied.

Then another barrage of missiles slammed into one of the enemy ships.

"Target their life support."

Almost at once, there was a massive explosion heard, then several smaller ones as fires erupted all over the enemy ships.

It won' t be long now; victory is mine, Nova thought. She could feel victory in her grasp. Her plans were going along just as she had expected, but there was more work she and her army would have to do. This was only the beginning.

"Scan the ship for damage and weak spots. Do it now."

"Scanning is complete. Life support is still functioning at full power. Navigation is as well, and weapons systems are at half power."

"Target their weapons systems."

"They are firing weapons at us. Evasive action is needed. We don't have time to target their weapons systems/' one of the crew announced.

"Move the ship out of range of their weapons and then target their weapons systems/' Nova ordered as her ship was hit with weapons fire.

Everyone in the cockpit was thrown to the floor. "Damage report!" Nova shouted as she tried to regain her composure.

"There are fires on several levels along with many breaches/' a crewmember reported.

"Seal off all the breached areas and put out the fires. How many casualties are there?" Nova asked.

"Thousands have perished."

A renewed hatred burned in her heart.

"Continue to target their life support, propulsion systems, and defense weapons."

Nova wanted to know who was flying the lead ship. Was it an Andromeda Force spy? Whoever it was had skills. How did the Grand Oracle find someone with such talent? Could it be a former military officer? Nova wanted to know because she wanted to kill the lead pilot and make an example of the pilot in a very public execution.

Nova pressed a button on her captain's seat arm rest and a three-dimensional image appeared. Studying the image for a moment, she noticed that they would arrive at Orion Nebula's secret base soon. It was her wish to destroy the oracle ships before that happened. It didn't look like it was going to happen, so Nova was running ideas around in her head.

"Find a weakness in their shields and fire on those spots. We need to overwhelm their systems so we can destroy their shields."

Nova watched as her ship attacked the two ships of oracles. She felt helpless to stop them from reaching Orion Nebula's base. But what else could she do? Her thoughts turned back again to the pilot of the first ship. Who was flying the ship and what training did this person have? Did Orion have a hand in training the pilot?

"Open a com link with the lead ship."

"The link is open now," a crewmember stated.

"I am Nova Spectrum. I will spare everyone's life if you agree to turn over your captain to me. There is no need for anyone else to die. Those who capture the captain will be rewarded. Failure to follow my wishes will result in more death. So I offer the life of one for the life of many. The time is now to decide what you will do. Is there anyone brave enough to save their own lives? You must give the pilot over to me before you reach your destination or all will die."

Nova didn't think anyone would mutiny against the pilot. It was an attempt to play with the loyalties of the crew. She hoped her offer would create division. Time would tell, but she knew the oracles would reach their destination soon. If that happened and the pilot wasn't turned over to her, Nova knew it would be problematic. She would have a harder time silencing

the oracles once they reached the base. But there were

plans for every scenario on her mind now.

"The enemy is about to leave a hyperspace

jump."

"Once we do as well, send out the fighters."

"We are ending a hyperspace jump now."

"Prepare my fighter and notify my students to

leave the ship in their fighters," Nova ordered as she

rose from her seat after taking in a glimpse of a world

on a view screen.

Chapter 11

Training and skill are the things Europa Comet had. The Grand Oracle had wanted her to learn how to fly and told her it was for the protection of the oracles. Now she was near Orion Nebula's secret base.

"Mother, this is Wing Leader. Our ETA is ten minutes and we're coming in hot with a pregnant daughter," Europa said as she radioed Orion's secret base.

"Hear you are coming for a visit. We will be expecting you in short order. Father out," the base commander, Randar Star, replied.

Knowing there was an enemy ship pursuing the oracles, he went to work preparing for the oracles' arrival.

Europa saw the base and a runway as she guided both ships of oracles down to the runway and into the base. The cargo bay doors were shut as the two spaceships continued to move at a snail's pace through a long tunnel. At the end of the tunnel was a docking bay. Once docked, Europa rose from her seat and left the cockpit. She opened the ship's door and led the oracles in her ship out. The sound of shuffling feet filled the base with noise.

The oracles in the second ship emerged as well.

Everyone was silent as the group moved behind

Europa. They walked down a wide staircase and into a

well-lit tunnel. Walking down the tunnel, they came to

a curve and followed it until they reached a heavy

security door. The security door opened and allowed

them to follow each other into a large room. There was

a strip of yellow lights in the ceiling, which were

blinking. Europa decided to follow the yellow lights

and they came to another security door. The door

opened to allow the group entry and they continued

their forward movement.

Europa had heard the base was massive, but she

couldn't fully comprehend the size and scope of the

base until now. The doors to the base were several feet

thick. In fact, they looked like blast doors that could withstand a nuclear attack. But as she led the oracles down a massive tunnel, she thought the doors wouldn't repel an attack from Nova Spectrum.

There was a bend in the hallway. Two massive doors opened, revealing another tunnel and a circular stairwell. Green lights along the wall of the stairwell lit up. Europa and company ran up the stairs and upon reaching the top, a door opened. Moving forward, the oracles followed a blue light down a tunnel to the left. The loud sound of their feet pounding on the wooden floor in the hallway was deafening. It sounded like a group of wild animals stampeding. There was no time for rest, Europa knew. The oracles had prepared for this day. Looking behind her, no one seemed winded or on the verge of collapse. Fear and adrenaline compelled them to move forward. Hope that they would escape was also alive in their hearts and minds, Europa thought.

The hallway they stood in now ended. A door opened to a room with several doors. A yellow light came on above a door and when it opened Europa led the way down a narrow, steep, slanting, dark hallway. At the end of the hallway a door opened, and Europa saw a narrow metal walkway high up from a floor below. In a room below were rows of computer banks lining the walls on either side. She didn't see anyone working on the computers and thought it was odd. But then again, she realized the base was under attack.

After leaving the walkway, Europa came to a room with lasers situated at various angles. She stood there as laser beams were turned off one at a time. Once all of the laser beams were deactivated, Europa advanced after a door opened and she walked onto another metal walkway. This one was wide. This room was hot. Looking over the edge, she saw steam rising from machines producing heat.

The walkway ended above the middle of the room below. It took a few moments, but another walkway rose from the room below to attach to where Europa was now standing. This walkway was T-shaped. Red lights lit up. Europa moved to the left, following the red light, and the journey continued deeper into the base.

The metal walkway led to a hallway with a concrete floor. On both sides of the hallway were doors with medical signs. As Europa ran past the doors, she noticed that the medical wing of the base was empty. She wondered where the base personnel were at this moment. But then she realized the base was massive and there were a lot of areas to defend. At the end of the hallway they came to a massive door that looked like it could withstand a nuclear blast. The door opened and to Europa's amazement, it was a massive room filled with weapons neatly stacked on racks in caged in areas. The door to the cages opened, allowing the oracles access to the weapons.

"Take as many weapons as you can carry. We will rest until all of you have weapons," Europa announced as she walked over to a row of weapons and took weapons for herself. Then she walked out of caged area and waited for the other oracles. It took only a few minutes for the oracles to each grab their weapon of choice.

Europa then led the oracles to a blast door as massive as the one when they'd entered the room and waited a moment for it to open. Once the door opened, Europa ran into a gigantic room filled with military vehicles of all types and shapes. The smell of oil, grease, and fuel lingered in the air. At the end of the room there was a huge elevator. The elevator doors opened and when all the oracles entered, the doors closed. Europa could feel the elevator descend at a steady pace. She wondered how much more of the base they would have to explore before meeting the base commander. The descent seemed to last for hours, but it finally stopped moving.

The elevator doors opened to reveal a massive underground tunnel that seemed to go on forever. A string of red lights lit up along one side of the tunnel. Once all of the oracles left the elevator, the doors closed and Europa led the group down the tunnel. She noticed the floor and walls were as smooth as glass. The only sound was the pounding of their feet as they ran down the length of the tunnel. They came to a T intersection, and the group stopped for a moment as the red light went out and green lights turned on straight ahead of them in a high ceiling.

Europa led the group down this tunnel, hoping their journey would end soon and they would be safe. She was filled with hope that this base would save their lives. But she also knew Nova Spectrum was nearby and posed a constant threat.

A yellow light lit up in the ceiling above a door, then the door opened. The oracles entered to see a large, empty room. When the door behind them closed, a door opened in front of them. This room was larger and just as empty. In front of the group a red light came on. This time a voice was hear over a loudspeaker.

" Welcome to the base. Please move forward to the next room."

Europa and the group stood in front of the door and waited for it to open.

Chapter 12

Strategic plans were floating around in Nova Spectrum's mind as she flew around Orion Nebula's secret base in her fighter. The threat was the ground forces, and the need was to take them out.

"Take out the ground forces at once and capture the base," Nova ordered her students.

Nova and her students flew past the ground forces as they fired off missiles. Massive explosions were heard, and fires were erupting everywhere around the impact site.

Nova peppered the area with bombs and fired her laser cannons at those on the ground who fought back. Repeatedly, bombs rained down and laser cannons were fired. After what seem like hours, there was silence on the ground and the carnage of bodies ripped apart. Smoke rose into the air as fires spread. The smell of blood and death were in the air.

Then, when it looked like Nova had won, reinforcements arrived. The reinforcements had heavy, powered lasers and missile launchers. The ground forces activated shield generator disks. The generator disks floated about, protecting the soldiers and their equipment.

A wave of fighters came down, shooting at the soldiers. But the protective barrier from the shield generators protected them. The soldiers wasted no time and returned fire, destroying the fighters. Then they got ready to take on Nova and her students.

Nova came down and fired her weapons while her students did the same. Nova's ship was hit, spiraled out of control, and hit the ground. The ship took an angry gouge out of the ground.

Nova pressed a button on the control panel in front of her and ejected out of her fighter ship. Moments later, it exploded. A parachute opened up and she landed on the ground outside of Orion's secret base. Nova unbuckled herself from the cockpit seat, then activated her death ball and her death wand and started walking through thigh-high deep snow. She knew soldiers would come to investigate the crash site, so she wanted to be ready.

"I survived the crash landing. Now you must take out the shield generators around the base. They are a hazard preventing us easy entry into the base itself. Follow in close formation and attack. Send squadrons of fighters to the surface to assist me," Nova instructed as she spoke to her students through a com link.

Then she walked closer to enemy soldiers, who were fighting her forces.

She watched as her students attacked the shield generators. Then she came under attack from soldiers on the ground. Her death ball struck many of them down, denying them the chance to kill Nova. Those who got past the death ball came charging at her. With ease, Nova sliced the soldiers in half with the use of her death wand.

The sounds of war filled her ears, and the smell of blood was present where Nova walked. She came upon soldiers protected by shields, giving them a protective barrier. She stared into their worried faces for a moment as some of them shot blasters at her. With the wave of a hand, the blaster fire missed her. Then she brought her death wand down, hitting the force field surrounding the soldiers. At once, the shield came down and Nova rushed forward, slicing through the soldiers in the blink of an eye. One threat she destroyed, but several remained for Nova to wipe out.

"We must find the control room at once since I'm sure this base is being prepared to self-destruct at this moment," Nova Spectrum informed her students, Denog Serpens, Yospher Ejecta, and Grifwid Gravity. Enemy troops loyal to Nova Spectrum opened the doors to Orion's secret base. As soon as they entered, a fierce gun battle erupted everywhere but they advanced. Nova Spectrum held up her hands, as did her students. They walked past the base security, using magic to repel any gunfire.

Then they quickened their pace down a long corridor.

Nova stopped walking as a metal door barred the way forward. Reaching into a pocket, she threw a small metal ball into the air. It was her death ball. At once, blood-red laser beams fired from the ball, hitting locked doors and killing base security. She noticed her students did the same. In no time at all the doors were blown apart and Nova moved forward, letting her death ball do her bidding.

Nova enjoyed seeing Yospher killing base security. She stopped moving forward when both Denog and Grifwid held base security alive.

"Yospher, continue your killing spree and enjoy," Nova commanded with a smile.

Then Nova moved forward to where Denog and Grifwid stood. She looked at the base security for a moment. Nova held up her hands and all the security soldiers rose from the floor, hovering high above the floor.

"Tell me where the control room is and I will spare your lives. Remain silent and you die. The choice is yours to make."

Silence filled the area where Nova stood. "Kill them."

Denog and Grifwid activated their death wands and sliced the base security in half. When they were dead, Nova lowered her hands and moved forward down the corridor. Denog Serpens' silver eyes were focused on hatred, Nova thought. His left hand was a burning blood-red flame that glowed in the hallway. He wore a long, white cloak. Grifwid Gravity wore a green cloak. It pleased Nova that Grifwid was all business and seemed to enjoy killing as much as she did.

While Yospher went off on her own deeper into the base, Nova and her other two students were swiftly advancing as well. The base security was no match for Nova and her students. As long as the battle raged, it gave the oracles the chance to flee, and this was what Nova wanted to prevent.

Chapter 13

Survival was on Europa Comet's mind as she met the base commander of Orion Nebula's secret base, who was duty bound to help the oracles. She knew the oracles represented truth and justice.

Europa and the oracles entered a large room. Soldiers were standing with an impressive array of weaponry. One man stood in front of the others.

"Europa Comet, I am the commander of this base. My name is Randar Star."

"I'm pleased to meet you, Commander Star," Europa said as she took the commander's hand in a strong handshake of greeting and friendship.

Europa's eyes focused on the man in front of her, who was a young man of medium height with the build of a fighter. He had blue hair and white eyes. He had silver skin covering his body and a mechanical right hand.

"Battle scar?" Europa asked, looking at his mechanical hand.

"You could say that. It happened during Operation Killjoy. Orion Nebula saved my life in more ways than one."

"It seems Orion is someone special, and in certain circles he is all people talk about," Europa stated.

"All I can say is that these days he has more enemies than friends. We can talk about him later. But now I'd break out the best wine we have, but we don't have time for this. Nova Spectrum has entered the base. We must evacuate all the oracles from this base now. We need to hurry. Get into small groups of five and jump into the transport shuttles. We will then place you on different ships and leave at once,"

Commander Randar Star informed as he watched the transport shuttle arrive.

The transport shuttle had one wheel in the front and two in the back. It resembled a small pyramid and could seat six.

One after another, transport shuttles were loaded. They sped away down long tunnels and passageways, arriving at waiting ships, which were powering up and prepared for a quick evacuation.

Commander Star and Europa both agreed they would take the last shuttle. After all, Europa had a duty to make sure the oracles were safe. She couldn't bear the thought of Nova killing any of the young girls she had come to know and love.

As the oracles entered, the waiting ships' pilots were running preflight plans. The pilots were also looking at last-minute classified secret documents. They didn't know where they were to fly the oracles until they opened the secret documents. After entering the coordinates into the ship's flight plan, they put the secret documents into a slot on the side of the control panel. The documents were then burned.

Training and leadership were the reasons why the oracles were getting away to safety. Spaceships were leaving the base on a rigorous schedule. Once they left the base, they went into a hyperspace jump. Their orders were to land on specific planets scattered throughout the galaxy. Half of the base security decided to stay behind fighting Nova Spectrum. The other half left with the oracles due to the constant threat of danger and need for protection. Europa took the last ship as it finally arrived. With her was Orion's friend Commander Star. It was just the two of them plus a pilot. Moments later, the shuttle sped down a long corridor that led to where the spaceships were housed in a hangar wing.

The shuttle stopped and the pilot led the pair to a spaceship. The pilot entered the cockpit while Europa and Commander Star took a seat, putting on safety belts. Their ship lifted off the floor of the hangar bay, leaving the base behind and entering space.

"Don't worry. I set the base to self-destruct, so she won't have the base for long," Randar said, trying to comfort Europa.

"We are in your debt on this day, and your sacrifice to protect the oracles we will not forget," Europa responded as tears rolled down her face.

"It's all a shame."

"What is?"

"I've worked at several bases, but this one is my favorite. Now I fear I'll never see it again. Do you see a bright future for me?" Randar asked.

Europa closed her eyes for a long moment as the ship they were in left the base and entered a hyperspace jump. She was silent for what seemed like hours.

"I see your path. It is clear to me. You are a man of action, a warrior or fighter. You will move around often; danger will follow you. Mighty deeds you will do. Your list of friends will grow, as well as your list of enemies. Later you will regain the base you just lost and command it again. You will also win a decisive battle at the base, which will turn the tide of war in the favor of justice."

"I will do all that in one or two days?" Star asked

Both of them started laughing at the same time.

"It will take place at the right time. Now, how about that drink you promised me? You want to make a good first impression, don't you?"

Star seemed to blush. He touched a button beside him and a door opened. He grabbed two champagne glasses. Then he reached for tongs and placed ice in both glasses. After that, he pressed another button and another door opened. He took out a bottle of champagne, opened the bottle, and poured it in each glass.

Raising her glass, Europa said, "To the safety and long life of the oracles."

Star picked up his glass and replied, "To meeting new friends."

They both clinked their glasses together and took a sip of the champagne.

"Do you know where Orion is now?" Europa asked.

"No. I don't think anyone does. When he needs me, Orion will contact me."

Chapter 14

Candar Mensa was lying on the bottom of an ocean on planet Bormino. It was Nova Spectrum who had pushed her into the ocean when they fought and had also thrown a concrete slab on top of her. The situation now was dire. Candar created an air bubble around her head so she could breathe. She also used her training and magic to lift the concrete slab an inch away from her body. Candar was finding it hard to concentrate since she had been in the water for a few hours now. She feared she would run out of air. Then she had an idea. Candar let out a cry similar to a whale call.

It didn't take long for her to hear a response. A pair of whales came to the rescue of Candar and moved the concrete slab Nova had placed on top of her. She wanted to take the battle to Nova and knew she would have to steal a spaceship to get off the planet. The whales helped lift her to the surface of the ocean, and then she ran on top of the water right to the shoreline. Once on dry land, a guard attacked her. Candar lost no time shooting him. She didn't see him fall to the ground dead because her eyes were on a fighter ship protected by several guards.

Candar needed a distraction since there were too many soldiers surrounding the fighter ship she wanted to steal. Looking down at her feet, she found a few small pebbles. She picked them up in her hand and watched the activity in the room for a moment. Then she threw a pebble into the cargo bay. She watched as some of the soldiers broke off, moving away from the ship she wanted to steal. Next Candar took out her death ball and watched it float into the cargo bay, undetected. The death ball rose to the ceiling and then came down fast. White laser beams from the death ball attacked soldiers in the room.

Candar then opened fire on them with her blaster, moving forward and taking her death wand out of its sheath. As the death ball went to work killing her opponents with great speed, she charged forward with her death wand. She did her best to fend off the attacks coming from all sides as guards surrounded her. More guards entered the palace cargo bay. They surrounded the fighter ship Candar still had in her sight.

Nothing is ever easy, Candar thought as she fought for her survival. Using her death wand, she sliced through bodies like a knife slices through butter. All around her was carnage. The smell of blood was thick in the air. Severed bodies littered the floor. It was almost too much for her to take in now. Rage consumed her. A dark burning rage against Nova and her followers swelled up in her heart. This rage gave Candar the strength to push forward and fight those foolish enough to attack her.

Candar moved deeper into the cargo bay and away from the ship she wanted. She fought the soldiers with her death wand in one hand and fired her blaster at nearby ships, causing them to explode. This also caused several of the soldiers too close to the exploding ships to die. Some were thrown backwards, and others caught on fire. All of the mayhem attracted the attention of soldiers, who stormed into the room with weapons drawn.

Candar shot at the lighting in the room, sending the cargo bay into darkness. The only light in the room came from her death wand, death ball, blaster, and enemy blasters. Candar continued to shoot ships and other vehicles in an effort to destroy as much as she could.

Jumping to the floor, Candar avoided being shot as she watched two soldiers near her shoot each other. Then she crouched down by a fighter as an army of androids entered the chaos in the room. All the androids had lights attached to their helmets and heavy-duty blaster rifles. Candar knew it wouldn't take them long to scan for her body, so she put a plan into motion. She closed her eyes and concentrated on the ships in the room. At once, all of the ships in the room turned on and started firing weapons. The androids hit by the ship's weapons exploded, killing several soldiers near the blast site.

She didn't know how long she could control the ships with her mind. Candar was growing tired as a new group of soldiers arrived with high-powered blasters. As Candar was concentrating on controlling the ships, the new arrival of soldiers were firing on the ships, destroying them so they couldn't harm anyone.

Candar lost concentration and the ships stopped firing weapons on soldiers. She was growing tired. She watched her death ball kill soldiers about the room. Then she rose from her position and joined the fight, firing her blaster and using her death wand.

The soldiers moved in closer to her, as well as the androids that were still functioning. Candar slammed her death wand on the floor and this created shock waves, pushing the soldiers and androids back. Many never got up to fight again.

More soldiers arrived fresh to the fight. It seemed an endless sea of soldiers was lurking around the comer. Candar concentrated on the new soldiers and placed thoughts in their heads. The weak-minded soldiers from the new group stood around Candar and opened fire on soldiers, trying to kill her. Candar didn't know how long she could control the weak-minded soldiers, but for now it gave her a chance to stay alive for a few more minutes.

Devastator bombs were thrown near the soldiers protecting Candar. The bombs were called devastator bombs for a reason. They were powerful and created a huge impact crater. The blast from the weapons was like that of a strong hurricane. All of the soldiers protecting Candar perished. Some fell into the crater; others were killed by the blast. But Candar was safe. She used her powers to create a protective shield around herself, so the devastator bomb didn't harm her.

Growing tired of the battle, she didn't know how much longer she would last. The only thing helping her was the desire to fight for justice. Her protective shield disappeared. Her death ball moved about the room, taking out soldiers. But those near her she had to fight on her own. She put away her blaster and swung her death wand into the bodies of several soldiers, killing them instantly. Candar started to move closer to the ship she wanted to steal while fighting for her life.

Time seemed to pass in slow motion. She seemed to take a few steps closer to her exit then was forced to pull back. It all seemed hopeless, but she had to continue fighting. Just a little more time and she could leave this place and go after Nova's war machine. Taking out her blaster, she started shooting. Then she pressed a button on her death wand, and it lifted her up and into the open cockpit seat of the ship she wanted to steal.

Candar deactivated her death wand. She held out her hand for her death ball and it returned to her. The cockpit door closed. Next, she activated the ship's shield and turned on the engine. Candar turned on the weapons systems and moved the ship around a full three hundred and sixty degrees. She destroyed anything moving. Then she set a course for a

hyperspace jump. She hoped she would find Nova and

catch her off guard. Time was important now. The

oracles needed her protection. The ship flew out of the

room and out into space.

Chapter 15

Anger coursed through her veins as Candar Mensa arrived at Orion Nebula's secret base and she knew just what she wanted to do. She wanted to punish Nova Spectrum by causing as much damage as she could inflict while flying above the base. She had a strategy she wanted to put into action.

Flying in a fighter, she fired at a large battleship, hoping to hit it just right. A small explosion erupted from the spot she hit. Then she fired off a missile, pulling away from the ship as fast as she could. The battle cruiser shook as explosions erupted. Soon the ship started to break apart. This caused injury to other battle cruisers too close in formation. Several other ships were hit with big chunks of the battle cruiser. These ships broke apart, causing a domino effect to other ships as they erupted. The battle cruisers frantically tried to pull out of formation but many of them couldn't do it in time. Those ships that couldn't pull away created black smoke, fireballs, and falling debris in the sky all around the base.

The debris from the destroyed ship started raining down, littering the landscape and falling on Nova's and Orion's soldiers, who were engaged in fierce battles. The battle was just underway, Candar thought, but there was still more she could do. Her focus was to destroy as many battle cruisers as she could.

All this destruction caused several fighters to break off from the fight to follow Candar's ship in hot pursuit. Now she had a new worry. She hoped to cause more damage before any enemy fighter damaged her ship. There were also soldiers on the ground who needed help, and she wanted to provide it.

"I am the Light Bearer signing in. Is anyone on the ground in need of help? Please respond now," Candar announced.

There was an explosion of chatter as several soldiers on the ground pleaded for help. Candar adjusted her flight path and descended to the surface, flying low above the ground. She fired on what she thought were Nova's forces while keeping track of the fighters shooting at her. The soldiers on the ground hit a few of the fighters trailing Candar.

Then she went on to the next group of soldiers in need of help. Some of the fighters attacking her were shot down by ground forces loyal to Orion. But as soon as the enemy fighters were shot down, more fighters followed close behind Candar.

Seeing a group of soldiers below her that were pinned down, Candar came to the rescue, destroying the soldiers and weapons standing in the way of

Orion's advancing soldiers. As she flew by, soldiers waved to her and she felt their deep gratitude. But she was brought back to reality when the fighters on her tail almost hit her ship. There were now more fighters tailing her than she could count. Candar pushed her fighter to the limit in an effort to break away from the enemy fighters. But they kept up with her. This was when ground forces loyal to Orion Nebula started shooting at the fighters trailing Candar. Several fighters were hit and crashed on the ground, but one fighter remained. *The pilot had skill,* Candar thought. She flew higher in the clouds in an attempt to hide, but the enemy fighter was still firing at her ship.

Candar flew out of the cloud layer and down to a large battle cruiser on a collision course with the cockpit. The enemy fighter kept pace with her, firing weapons. The gap between Candar's ship and the battle cruiser narrowed. Candar had her hand on the ship's guns and was about to fire when her ship was hit by the fighter following her. She recovered with lightning speed, firing her weapons at the cockpit of the battle cruiser, and pulled away from the ship moments before impact.

Alarms were going off on the dashboard of Candar's ship. She wanted to assess the damage but the enemy fighter was still with her. There was no place to hide. Candar planned an escape route, seeing several enemy fighters before her. She flew close to the ships and blew one up. This created a debris field. Candar waited a moment then flew down away from the debris field, but the ship that was following her was hit. She didn't know the extent of the other fighter, but for the moment she was free to go back to fighting Nova's war machine.

Despite the alarms and warning signals coming from her ship's cockpit display, Candar didn't want to give up the fight just yet. But she also knew the ship couldn't withstand more damage. Looking over the damage to her ship, she decided the damage wasn't yet critical.

Seeing a cluster of enemy fighters before her, she opened fire. The fighters were transformed into fireballs and slammed into large battle cruisers. This was rewarded by huge explosions as the battle cruisers started to fall to the planet below.

Just when Candar was starting to feel good about how things were going, the enemy pilot, who had been trailing her before, returned, peppering her ship with weapon fire. Candar flew her fighter down to tree level, hoping to lose her attacker. When she found the enemy pilot was still with her, she flew below the tree line, trying to avoid crashing into a building.

A new problem occurred when enemy forces on the ground started shooting at her ship in an effort to take it down. She moved to the right then to the left as weapons fired from below. Candar fired off her own weapons and huge explosions erupted on the ground. But then her ship was hit from behind. Candar's dashboard lit up and her ship dropped lower to the ground as explosions were going off. Closing her eyes, she calmed herself down. She concentrated on stopping the ship from spinning. Then Candar focused on the ship rising higher into the air. Opening her eyes, she saw on the control board in front of her that the enemy fighter was still trailing her.

Candar pulled the ship higher and set her fighter on a collision course with a battle cruiser. The enemy fighter continued to fire weapons at her, but she was determined to survive. The gap between Candar and the battle cruiser narrowed. She could see the cockpit of the battle cruiser and the worried faces of those present. Candar fired off a missile and pulled away from the battle cruiser. The fighter behind her was hit by pieces of the battle cruiser. Meanwhile, Candar flew in a loop and was behind the enemy fighter. She opened fire and hit the fighter. She watched as it blew up.

Candar was going back to the battle when she noticed the ship's weapons systems were not working. Either there were no more weapons on her ship or the damage was preventing the weapons systems from working. Without weapons she had to leave the area. She was satisfied that she had destroyed several battle cruisers but disappointed she didn't get them all. Candar knew Nova would replace all of the battle cruisers that were now destroyed overnight. She then plotted a hyperspace jump and left the battle. She hoped her fighter could make it to a repair station. She didn't want to die in this fighter, and she was worried.

Chapter 16

Yospher Ejecta, one of Nova Spectrum's students, was still fighting Orion Nebula's security forces. She thought she was deep into the base by now, but the booby traps and security forces hampered her from moving forward faster than she wanted to move. At every turn, Yospher had to use caution and even though she had powers, she could still die.

Her back was against a wall in a hallway. She held her death wand in one hand, a blaster in the other hand, and her death ball floated before her. Pressing a button on a wall opened a door. Yospher sent her death ball forward to enter the room. She waited a moment and heard blasters going off and the cries of men dying. Then she entered the room to see dead bodies littering the floor. The room was circular with a balcony and several doors on an upper level. At once the doors opened and soldiers rushed out onto the top balcony, firing blaster rifles. Yospher hit a button on her death wand, and it lifted her into the air. She fired her blaster as her death ball rose to the top balcony and started shooting laser beams at the enemy soldiers. By the time she reached the top balcony, there was just one soldier left to take care of. Yospher blocked the soldier's blaster fire with her death wand and charged forward, slicing him in half. Now she stood alone on the balcony and braced herself for what was behind the doors all around her.

Yospher pressed a button on her flight suit and a three-dimensional display of the base appeared at eye level. After a moment, she decided to walk over to a red door. Pressing a button on a wall opened the door. Yospher's death ball floated ahead of her, ready to strike anyone. Entering a large room, Yospher stood for a moment, scanning the room for enemies to kill. When she didn't see anyone, she walked down a flight of stairs to a floor below.

"Yospher checking in," she announced to her com link.

"Where are you right now?" Nova Spectrum asked.

Yospher looked around the room for a moment. "It looks like the communication room."

"Is the room secure?"

"For the moment I'm the only one in this room alive."

"Good, now send word that we need help on all clandestine channels. The sooner we can take full control of this base, we can use it to our advantage. Can you see where our enemies are gathered?"

"Yes, Nova, all video surveillance is still operational."

"I want updates on where Orion's forces are so we can kill them."

"I will do as you ..."

"Yospher, are you alright?"

"Nothing I can't handle ..."

Yospher turned away from a computer monitor right before it blew up. All lights in the room went dark. She wasn't alone anymore. Her death ball was moving about the room, firing an orange laser beam at enemy soldiers. The sound of men and women dying filled the large room. It was now time for her to go to work and Nova's orders would have to wait.

She pulled her death wand out of its sheath, straining her ears to pinpoint where her enemies were moving about the room. Several blasters went off at once as Yospher blocked them with her death wand. Then soldiers came rushing at her from all sides while her death ball was busy elsewhere. Yospher jumped down to the floor as the soldiers moved closer to her, and she sliced through their legs with ease. As the soldiers started falling, Yospher rose from the floor, shooting her blaster in one hand and swinging her death wand in the other.

A flash grenade exploded near where Yospher was standing, blinding her. She had to rely on her training, firing her blaster where she sensed her enemy stood. Still blind, several soldiers came forward, firing blasters as Yospher blocked the enemy fire with her death wand. Then she made a sweeping one hundred eighty-degree turn, slicing down her enemy. At last, there was silence and her vision returned to her.

"Yospher, I need you ..." Nova started saying.

But Yospher didn't hear a word. Her eyes were transfixed on a floating one hundred twenty-inch video screen that was as thin as a piece of paper. Tears fell from her eyes as she watched Candar Mensa destroying ship after ship. The thought of all of her friends dead hit her hard.

"Yospher, are you there?"

Yospher didn't respond. She had one goal in mind now. She left the room and ran down to the cargo bay. Yospher was filled with the desire to bring punishment and death to Candar for destroying ships and killing so many of her friends. She had her plans in order and intended to carry them out. Nothing would stand in her way.

Picking up a space helmet off a rack in a hallway, she put it on. Then she walked into the cargo bay, where she chose a small fighter and entered the cockpit. Being a young woman, she looked into a mirror and noticed the helmet fit well over her fox face. But still she worried someone would notice her and prevent her from flying out of the base. Or a worse situation was if she was prevented from leaving and was reported to Nova under guard. She was wearing a white spacesuit with a white cloak and hoped people would focus on what she was wearing instead of who she was.

"Code name Exterminator, I seek clearance for departure. Powering up now; preflight check is green," Yospher stated as she looked at the control panel in front of her and was waiting for the command to leave.

"Control to Exterminator, you have clearance to leave. Please get in a holding pattern along the blue line. Have a safe flight."

Without saying a word, Yospher positioned her ship into the right holding pattern. Then she waited for a light to turn green. When it did, she powered up her engines and left the base.

Yospher would get the chance at revenge soon, she thought. She couldn't wait to see the look on Candar Mensa's face moments before she killed her foe. Flying past the wreckage of damaged ships made it difficult for Yospher. She broke down in a steady stream of tears. All she could do now was remember the names of her friends and picture their faces in her mind. Intense anger flooded into her heart and all her tears dried up as she plotted a course to follow Candar.

Chapter 17

Candar Mensa sat alone in a fighter she had

stolen from the Grand Oracle's castle, which was now

under the control of Nova Spectrum. The light in the

cockpit was dim and fading fast. Candar hoped to

reach a repair station she knew was in the area. But the

ship's systems were failing. She might not make it the

repair station. Pushing her worries aside, Candar

looked around the dashboard. Several red lights were

blinking. Alarms were blaring, giving Candar a

throbbing headache. She couldn't give in to despair. Candar forced herself to stay optimistic. She didn't want this ship to be her metal coffin. Candar preferred to die in a duel or battle.

"Computer, reroute energy to navigation systems," Candar ordered.

"If this is done, some systems will fail," the computer responded.

"I will take the risks. Now do as I say," Candar ordered.

"Rerouting energy to navigation is now complete," the computer responded.

A series of red blinking lights lit up on the dashboard in front of Candar. She noticed that fuel was leaking from the ship. Then the light in the cockpit went dark. So Candar had to fly the ship by memory.

"Life support is failing/' the computer announced.

The repair station came into view. Candar hoped she would make it to the repair station. It loomed large in her view port window. She hied to stay calm.

"Life support is down to fifty percent and failing/' the computer announced.

Fire broke out here and there as Candar Mensa flew her ship closer to the repair station.

"I need permission to land. I have small fires in the cockpit and the landing gear has malfunctioned. Multiple systems are down and life support is failing."

"Control to the approaching ship. You are coming in too fast. You can't dock. Fly around the space station and try again. If you can slow down, go to the docking bay nine straight ahead."

Candar flew past the docking bay and around the repair station. She flew the ship even though the smoke in the cockpit rose, making it difficult to see. Candar put on an oxygen mask and closed her eyes, trying to slow the ship down with her mind. All at once, her instrument panel malfunctioned and everything went blank.

Using her mind, she slowed the ship down, but it was still moving too fast for a safe landing. She entered the cargo bay, but the landing gear still wasn't working. The ship slammed onto the deck and sped across the floor. A shower of sparks flew about, almost hitting another ship. Candar's ship spun around and around before coming to a complete stop.

A group of men and women rushed to Candar's ship. Some worked on putting out fires while others worked on opening the hatch door. It took several minutes, but they opened the hatch door and Candar emerged unscathed.

"Do you need medical attention? We have an excellent medical wing, which is the pride of this station. I can lead the way," one woman announced.

"I don't need medical attention. All I need is another ship."

"What kind of ship do you have in mind?"

"I will take the fastest ship you have. Make sure it has all the latest weaponry and is stocked with as much ammo as it can lift. I will also need several months' worth of food."

"And what do you want us to do with this ship? There will be a storage fee."

"I will sell it to you for scrap metal. The weapons onboard I will sell to you as well."

"You will receive a lofty price for the ship and any weapons onboard, but it won't be enough to cover the cost of a new ship."

"I understand."

"How will you pay the difference?"

"I will pay you triple your normal rate if you work around the clock. I need a new ship as soon as possible. Do we have an understanding?"

"Yes. You are most generous, but our rates are higher than most repair stations."

"Money is no problem, but my time is valuable."

"We will get you a new ship. What is your name?"

"Candar Mensa. What will a new ship cost me?"

"First we must weigh your ship. Then we can determine how much to pay you for your damaged ship. The weapons on board your ship will be weighed and evaluated so we can get a price for that as well."

"When will you have a new ship for me?"

"Normally it takes several weeks to completely build a ship from design to finish. But you are in luck. We are in the final stages of completing a ship. You can have it for the right price. How will you pay?"

"I will pay in gold coins. How long will it take?"

"A few hours at most; that is, if we don't run into any problems."

"How will you contact me?"

"Here, take this com. I will let you know when your new ship is ready."

After taking the com, Candar turned to the women she had been talking to. "I need lodging. It has been a long day and I need to rest. I will need some

food prepared as well when I wake up."

"I will arrange a room for you. As for food, there

is a grand buffet open twenty-four hours a day. You

can get food there and it is really good food."

The woman walked away and then came back

with a key. "If you will follow me, I will show you to

your room."

Candar followed the woman a short distance to

a hallway, where there were rows of doors on either

side. They stopped at a door in the middle of the

hallway.

"This is your room. Don't worry about any

noise. Once you close your door, you won't hear

anything. We have taken special planning to make sure noise suppression is not a problem for our guests. Working on the floor putting together a spaceship is very noisy. Can I get you anything else?"

"No. Thank you for your help."

When the woman walked away, Candar opened the door to her room and let it close by itself. She was so tired she didn't bother to change clothes. She walked over to a bed as the lights dimmed and she fell asleep instantly.

Chapter 18

Nova Spectrum was now at Orion's base. She had taken it over. The dead had been removed throughout the massive base. Now she and her forces could walk freely about and not have to worry about being shot at.

Nova walked out of her makeshift office and down to a row of prison cells. She needed information and the Grand Oracle was the only one who could provide it. A guard stood outside the

Grand Oracle's cell. When the guard saw Nova approaching, he unlocked the door to the cell. Nova walked into the cell and slapped the Grand Oracle in the face, hard. The Grand Oracle, who had been asleep, woke up.

Nova turned to the guard and said, "Leave us, but stay close by. I need to speak to the Grand Oracle in private."

Without saying a word, the guard left the cell, closing the door behind him, and walked down the hall out of earshot.

The Grand Oracle was chained to a wall with restraints around her wrists. There were also chains on the floor and restraints around her ankles. Now wide awake, she was prepared for anything Nova was about to do.

"You know why I am here so don't waste my time."

"I could say you are wasting my time," the Grand Oracle retorted.

"Tell me about the freedom fighters on your planet."

"Are these chains necessary? Are you afraid of me?"

"Give me my information."

"Yes, you are afraid of me, an old woman, I can see it in your eyes."

"Stop with your distractions and give me the information I seek."

"Or what? You will kill me?"

"I will kill you if you continue to waste my time."

"You won't kill me because I am more valuable to you alive."

Nova's face turned red with anger, the Grand Oracle noticed. Then she watched as Nova pulled out her death wand and held it inches from the Grand Oracle's face.

"Now tell me what I want to know or I will kill you here and now."

"I know nothing."

"Don't play me for a fool. Tell me all about the freedom fighters on your planet or I will use my death wand on you."

"You are such a disappointment. You could have been a great champion of peace and justice, but you have fallen from grace. You, Nova, have become a monster. You will never achieve your evil goals."

Nova brought her death wand closer to the Grand Oracle's face, cutting into it. "There will be a scar."

"I don't fear you and I don't fear death, but you do."

"We shall see how brave you are," Nova said as she put her death wand back in a sheath.

Nova reached into a pocket and threw her death ball into the air, where it hovered above the Grand Oracle's body.

"I believe you know what this is. Now every time you don't answer me, a laser beam will hit you. Tell me about the freedom fighters."

"You will never know what you seek about them."

Nova's death ball fired a laser beam at the Grand Oracle. She let out a cry of pain that seemed to satisfy Nova, who smiled.

"How many freedom fighters are there? Where are their bases?"

"There are too many to count. They are like grains of sand on a beach. Do you know how many grains of sand are on a beach?"

"Where are their bases?"

"In every sector of every galaxy; even you can't wipe them out."

"Give me specific locations to their bases. Do it now."

"If you want to find their bases, look no further than the planets you have conquered. You create a never-ending sea of freedom fighters."

"Wrong answer," Nova said as the death ball hit the Grand Oracle again with a laser beam.

The Grand Oracle moaned in pain. "Killing me will not benefit you."

"I will be the judge of that. Now tell me what weapons the freedom fighters have."

"They have weapons more powerful than you can imagine."

"Stop being so cryptic and answer me."

"They have justice on their side and hope. Those are the weapons you will never destroy."

Nova's death ball moved over to the Grand Oracle and fired a laser beam at her, hitting her in the chest. The smell of burnt flesh filled the room. A muffled cry came from the Grand Oracle.

"Nova, Yospher is not on this base. We searched every room," one of Nova's commanders reported.

"Thank you, commander, for the valuable information. Keep me posted on any further developments."

The Grand Oracle saw a change in Nova's facial expressions. She looked beyond angry with a mixture of deep concern.

"Where is Yospher?"

"She is not here with you?"

"Don't play with me. Did she visit you? If she isn't on this base then where is she? Death will come to you if you don't answer my questions. You must know it is foolish to fight me since I am more resilient than you," Nova Spectrum hissed in anger.

"As I have told you, I am not your prisoner. I will stay with you for a short while. But it was a choice I have made," the Grand Oracle stated in a calm voice with her eyes closed.

"Only a fool would think you weren't my prisoner. Now I will ask you again, where is my student, Yospher Ejecta? Also, tell me what you know about the Freedom Fighters on your home world?"

"Death will come to your student and she will face swift justice. Evil never triumphs. About the Freedom Fighters, you will never know what you seek. The path you travel now will lead to your own death."

The Grand Oracle smiled as she opened her eyes, showing no hint of fear.

"Did you tell Yospher where to find Candar Mensa?"

"Yospher has a date with death. It is a punishment for choosing the wrong path in life."

"I have had enough of your riddles. Tell me what I want to know or you die."

"You will not kill me. As I have said, I am too valuable to you alive for you to kill me. I don't fear death, but you do."

"I will make you give me the information."

"When you reach Yospher, you will arrive too late to save her from a death she deserves."

Chapter 19

Candar knew Yospher was now present on the repair station as she waited for a ship to finish being built. Candar could feel Yospher nearby and the full wall of intense hatred directed at her. She was calm and ready for a fight to the death.

Candar stood on a high bridge with a long drop to the next level below. She stood waiting and ready.

"Candar Mensa, you are under arrest!" Yospher shouted as she stood with the space station security.

"If I were you, I would not get involved in this fight," Candar said, her voice cool and steady as she stood with her back to the growing mob.

Candar noticed space station security standing on the edge of the bridge in front of her.

"This fight is no concern of yours. Pay no attention to us," Candar said as she watched the space station security in front of her move away.

"Skill will not save you or your magic. You are mine. You are dead," Yospher uttered with the menacing danger of a young woman on the verge of losing all her self-control.

She threw her death ball at her opponent. It fired blue laser beams at Candar, but she blocked the blows with her death wand.

Candar reached into her flight suit and her death ball hovered in the air. Yospher's death ball fired several laser beams at Candar[7] s death ball in an attempt to destroy it. Then Candar sliced Yospher's death ball in half and it fell to the floor of the bridge, a smoldering mess.

"You are no match for me," Candar informed with a hard edge in her voice as she blocked all efforts to kill her.

Candar and Yospher stared at each other. They both had their death wand, a hand-held plasma sword weapon with many uses, in hand ready for a duel. Candar wasted no time. She raised her death wand to strike Yospher but she moved away in time to avoid a death blow. The death duel was just starting.

Yospher, the younger of the two, moved with a cat-like speed. She wasted no time slashing at Candar with her death wand. Candar moved away but wasn't as agile as her opponent. Candar attacked Yospher, and their death wands clashed and clashed again. Sparks flew about and a loud hissing sound was heard. They pranced around the bridge. Then Yospher, seeing an opportunity, pushed Candar against the edge of the bridge. Candar didn't have much room to move. All she could do was raise her death wand at eye level to block Yospher's death blows.

Candar's death ball hit Yospher and then she moved away from Candar in pain. Then she sliced through one part of the railing by Candar, as well as the other side. Yospher then kicked Candar in the chest as the railing gave way. Candar fell to the level below. She was in pain as Yospher jumped down to the same level near where Candar was lying on the bridge.

Yospher walked over to Candar and stood above her, raising her death wand ready to kill. " At last now it is time for you to die. I avenge the death of my friends that you have killed."

Candar's death ball hit Yospher with laser beams and she staggered backwards. This gave Candar the opportunity she needed. She sprang forward, clashing her death wand with her opponent's. But as they fought, Yospher grabbed a blaster from a belt around her waist and started shooting. Candar worked hard to block both the blaster fire and her opponent's death wand while continuing to keep pressure on Yospher. She hoped Yospher would make a mistake so she could end the duel.

It was at this time that the repair station security had taken notice of the fight. They stood on both ends of the bridge, ready to end the fight.

"Put down your weapons now and end this fight or you either will be arrested or killed," the head of the security force threatened.

Candar and Yospher acted as if they hadn't heard the threat from the station security force. They continued with their duel, attacking and counter-

attacking. Their death wands continued to clash,

sending sparks flying about the area where they

fought.

The head of security raised his hand, and the

bridge was filled with thousands of security drones

with built-in lasers. Before they could attack the pair,

Candar's death balls destroyed many of the drones but

not all. They had to break away from fighting each

other to destroy the drones. Then they resumed the

duel. But more drones arrived.

Base security on each end of the bridge opened

fire on Yospher and Candar. They had to move fast to

block the weapon fire and the drones from harming

them. Some of the security force moved in closer to the

dueling pair but Candar's death ball shot laser beams at the soldiers, killing them where they stood.

Candar was alarmed by how much attention the duel was attracting. The other problem was she was growing tired and needed to rest. She didn't know how much longer she could keep up the fight. Candar swung her death wand around and missed her opponent by a few inches. Then she fell to her knees as Yospher advanced, standing over her, ready to kill.

Candar pulled out her blaster and fired at Yospher, hitting her in the chest. Yospher staggered backwards. It was now that Candar rose from her knees and stood. Seizing this moment, Candar attacked as security forces fired weapons. Yospher blocked the attack once, then twice. Determined to end the duel, Candar swung her death wand, forcing

Yospher to move close to the edge of the bridge. Then

Candar struck at Yospher, slicing her in two at the

torso. The upper part of Yospher s′body fell on a

bridge below while the lower part of her body

slumped on the bridge where Candar stood. Candar,

with her death wand still activated, knew it was

time to leave.

Now that she was the lone threat, security

drones surrounded her. Security officers formed a

ring around Candar. She slammed the bottom of

her death wand on the floor of the bridge. The

shock wave destroyed the drones and pushed the

security forces to either end of the bridge. Many

were lying on the floor dead. Other security forces

were in no condition to continue the fight. Realizing it was time to leave, Candar fled from the bridge and started running through the repair station to see if her new ship was ready to leave. As she ran, Candar noticed some space station security had taken an interest in her. They shot blasters at her, and she had to fend them off with her death wand and death ball.

Closer and closer she came to the area where her ship was being constructed. But as she looked around, there was a growing security threat trying to kill her. She was tired and ready to collapse, but adrenaline was pumping through her body, preventing her from falling to the floor.

Candar reached the ship building area of the station as an army of security forces were trying to get to her. She swatted at a few drones, splitting them in half. Turning to a woman behind a desk, Candar asked, "Is my ship ready for me to take and leave this base?"

"You seem to have a following. But yes, your ship is ready we have just loaded the last armaments onto your ship. There is the matter of payment."

"As I have already stated, I will pay three times your going rate. I believe this is the correct amount of money I owe you," Candar said, reaching into her flight suit as she handed a bag of gold coins to the woman.

The woman opened the bag and her eyes were wide. Before she could say anything, Candar said, "Keep the change. Now where is my ship?"

"Your ship is straight ahead. It is the first ship across the walkway. Don't worry, I will inform the control tower you need a clear flight path."

"Thank you," Candar replied as her death ball returned to her and she raced across the walkway to her ship.

Once she entered, Candar activated the ship's shields. It was seconds later that the ship was hit with enemy weapons, but no damage came to the ship. Candar made her way to the cockpit and sat down in the pilot's seat. She turned on the engines and received a message.

"Control to departing ship, please stay in lane three and wait for the light to turn green. It should only take a moment."

Candar didn't know if this was a trick or stalling tactic but when the light turned green, she flew out of the space repair station and into open space. She made up her mind where she wanted to go. With the course set, she left the cockpit and entered a large room nearby that had an inviting bed. Once she was lying on the bed, she fell asleep as the ship entered a hyper space jump.

Chapter 20

Nova Spectrum sat alone in the cockpit of her
fighter. She was approaching the repair space station
where Candar and Yospher had fought. Her thoughts
were with Yospher. She didn't sense she was alive, just
like the Grand Oracle had predicted. Or was it all a lie
to get her away from her base? The Grand Oracle
couldn't be trusted. She thought the Grand Oracle
spoke in riddles and half truths. But at the same time,
the Grand Oracle was valuable to her at the moment.

Once she felt the Grand Oracle was no longer valuable, she would kill her and send fear to her enemies.

"Control to approaching ship, go to docking bay twenty-five and reduce your speed."

Nova slowed the ship down as she approached the right docking bay. She flew her fighter into the space station and landed her ship. Several people approached her ship as she opened the hatch door and stepped out onto a platform.

"Who are you?" an attended asked.

"You haven't heard of me?"

"No."

"Well, you will soon enough. I am Nova Spectrum."

"I'm pleased to meet you, Nova. Why are you on this station? Can we service your ship while you are here? Are you in need of a room?"

"I won't need a room since I can't stay long. You could refuel my ship for me while I conduct some business. That is all I need, and if you could tell me where your morgue is, I would be grateful."

"Wait here a moment," the woman said as she walked away from Nova and started barking orders at her crew.

"This is a big space station. It is easy to get lost, so let me guide you to the morgue."

Nova nodded her approval. Her guide walked across the vast cargo bay, alive with activity. The smell of oil and fuel swirled about in the air. The constant noise of ships being built or repaired assaulted Nova's ears. They walked out of the cargo bay and down a long corridor that led to an elevator. When the elevator doors opened, Nova and her guide stepped inside. The doors closed and the guide pressed a button on a control panel. The elevator started to descend. It seemed to descend for hours, in Nova's opinion. When the doors opened, the pair walked down a corridor to another elevator. Once inside this elevator, the doors closed and the elevator descended to the bottom level of the repair space station.

The doors opened and Nova followed her guide down a corridor. At the end of the hallway, they turned to the left and stopped halfway down the hallway. Directly in front of Nova there was a steel door and above it was the word Morgue. The guide entered a password and the door opened. Stepping inside the morgue, Nova felt cold air and found it pleasing to her. In front of them there was a long corridor that seemed to go on forever. All along the hallway were rooms on either side.

The guide walked over to a computer terminal. "Arc you looking for someone in particular who has passed away?"

"Yes. Her name is Yospher Ejecta. I wish to see her body."

"It will be gruesome to see this body. I heard she was cut in half with a death wand."

"I still want to see her body."

"I understand," the guide stated as she entered information at the computer terminal.

It took a few minutes for the information to come up. When it did, the guide left the computer terminal and walked down the corridor to the room where Yospher's body was being stored.

"You will find Yospher's remains in this room," the guide stated.

"Thank you for your help. I would like to take the body to my ship now," Nova announced.

"You will have to sign authorization papers before you can take the body."

"I will sign any papers I need just as long as I can take the body."

The guide walked over to a computer terminal and entered a code. Papers soon after printed. The guide then placed the papers on a desk in the hallway and Nova walked over to the desk to sign the papers. The door where Yospher's body was being kept opened. Nova walked into the room and felt a chill. She saw a body covered with a white cloth lying on a hover board. The guide pressed a few buttons on the side of the hover board, and it floated out of the room and into the hallway.

It took a few minutes for Nova to reach her ship. Once inside of her ship, she placed Yospher's body on a steel table. Pressing a button on the side of the hover board sent it out of the ship, where it would return to the morgue. Nova closed the hatch door to her ship. It had been refueled and was ready to leave the space station. Now was the time to bring Yospher back to life. Nova took the cloth off of Yospher's body and looked at it for the first time. Her body was split in two pieces above the belly button.

Nova reached into a box and took out crystals and candles. The candles hovered about above Yospher's body. Then she opened another box, taking out a heart that wasn't beating. A young girl's life was taken when her heart was cut out of her. The heart floated above Yospher's body. It would take magic to bring her back to life, but she still had time, Nova knew. She would use black magic to bring Yospher back from the dead. In many circles, the use of black magic was forbidden, but not for Nova.

One by one, the black candles were lit. Nova then placed the crystals on Yospher's body. She closed her eyes as she placed her hands on Yospher's chest. Next she started an incantation which would bring Yospher back to life.

The crystals turned black and emitted an eerie light. Then they rose into the air and moved back and forth, producing a low hum. The heart started to beat but turned black in color.

Nova focused on healing Yospher, and she could feel Yospher coming back to life. Nova opened her eyes and noticed Yospher was whole again. The heart, she noticed, disappeared from her eyes. She closed her eyes once more and opened them to hear Yospher taking in a deep breath. She opened her eyes, alive again.

"You're lucky I brought you back to life."

"Candar Mensa, she killed me."

"I know. Why did you leave the base without telling me first? You are no match for her now and will need special training to kill Candar."

"I am sorry for the trouble I have caused."

"You must heal now. I will deal with this matter later."

"I'm sorry."

"Rest now, Yospher. Rest and heal," Nova said in a soothing voice as Yospher fell asleep.

Candar Mensa was going to pay for what she did to Yospher. Nova wanted her dead.

Chapter 21

Candar was now wide awake and sitting in the cockpit of her new fighter. She had to honor her promise to Captain Asterism. But at the same time, she wasn't looking forward to her meeting with the captain's wife. Candar wished she had the captain's body, but she didn't even have that to bring to the captain's family. A planet loomed large in the view port window and Candar knew she would now be engaged in making her descent. Candar's ship passed a cloud layer and she saw a massive

modern-day space port appear before her eyes.

There were too many buildings of various sizes to

count. An endless sea of ships flew about the vast

area, some landing while others were taking off.

"Light Bearer seeking permission to land,"

Candar announced through a com link.

"Control towers to Light Bearer, proceed to

the coordinates I am sending to you now," a female

voice advised.

Candar looked at her control board and

entered the coordinates into her navigation system.

After setting the ship on auto pilot, she left the

cockpit, gathered her things in another room, and

walked down to the cargo bay door. The ship landed with a light, almost unnoticeable touch.

Opening the cargo bay door, Candar saw a greeting party.

"State your name and your business," a well-dressed female military official stated.

"I am Candar Mensa. My visit will be brief. I am here as a condolence call."

"Who died?"

"Captain Asterism. He died on a secret mission for the Grand Oracle. I barely survived myself."

"He was a great man, and he will be missed."

"Yes, I share your thoughts."

"Before you go, I want to confirm you are who you say you are. We must be careful; there is talk that war will break out soon. Now look into this scanner," the military official ordered, holding up an eye scanner.

Candar looked into the scanner and then stepped back.

"Now place your hand on this palm reader," ordered the military officer.

Candar did as she was told, then she pulled her hand away from the scanner.

"Welcome to Beta Pictoris C, Candar Mensa. If there is anything I can do for you, just ask."

"There is one thing I need."

"And what is that?"

"I need access to an aquila."

"Aquilas are temperamental beasts that take years to master."

"I have a way with beasts."

"Very well, follow me," the military official stated.

Candar walked a short distance to the opening of a cave. She stood at the entrance and created a short, guttural sound. Then, as if it was answering a call, an aquila slowly walked out of the cave and stopped in front of Candar. The beast was amazing, Candar thought. It was the size of three killer whales in body and length with a long neck, serpentine head, and large wings. It was sea green in color and had a pleasing smell about it. The beast lowered its head to allow Candar to walk up its neck to reach a saddle. Candar took a seat in the saddle and let out a cry that told the aquila it was time to leave the ground and fly.

"You will have to stop halfway to your destination since aquilas can't reach the top of the mountain you are going to."

"Understood," Candar answered back as the aquila rose into the air and flew away from all of the activity on the ground.

Candar felt the wind rush at her as the aquila rose higher into the air. It was cool and refreshing after being in her fighter for several hours. She could feel the beast's heartbeat and this was a comfort as well. It had been a long time since she had the chance to ride an aquila, and she thought there was no other experience that compared to this.

The massive wings of the aquila took Candar higher into the air and just below the cloud layer. Then it started its descent to the ground high up on a mountain. Candar could see the beast was fast approaching trees below. Then the aquila landed with a gentle touch in a wide clearing of trees. It lowered its neck and Candar rose from the saddle.

She slid down the beast's neck and stood on the ground. Before leaving the aquila, she turned to the beast and rubbed its head.

Turning away from the beast, Candar knew she would have to walk to her destination on a narrow path high up on a mountain. She had to be careful not to fall to her death. It was midday before she reached Captain Asterism's house. She stood outside and studied the house for several minutes. It was modern and well-kept. The house was a three-story structure with several breathtaking views. She liked the color as well. It was a dark blue color with a red tile roof.

Drumming up courage, she knocked on the door. The door opened and Candar saw an attractive woman with long, curly brown hair and

orange-grey eyes. Her young children were

hugging their mother.

"Candar Mensa," Captain Asterism's wife,

Aurora, said. Turning to her children, Aurora said,

"Run along, children, I need to speak to Candar

alone."

When the children moved away from Aurora,

she turned to Candar.

"May I come in?"

"No, you may not," Aurora replied angrily as

she stepped outside of her house and closed the

door behind her.

"Why are you here, Candar? Where is my husband? Do you have him on a mission with little chance for him to survive? It is because of you that I don't see my husband often. What mission is he on now and when will I see him?"

Tears welled up in Candar's eyes and streamed down her face. She couldn't look into Aurora's eyes. Instead, she looked at the ground.

"What is the matter with you? Can't you look at me?"

Candar raised her head and locked eyes with Aurora. "I am sorry, but Asterism is dead."

Candar fell to her knees, consumed in grief. She looked up at Aurora, who took a step back and was leaning against the door to her house.

"What? What are you saying?"

"He's gone and will never come back."

"I knew this day would come! You killed my husband! You killed him!" Aurora shouted loudly enough for the people at the space port down below to hear.

Consumed in anger, Aurora struck Candar on the right side of the head, then the left side. She continued to beat Candar, then one of the children came outside.

"Mama, why are you hitting her?"

"Go inside now!"

When the young boy returned to the inside of the house, Aurora fell to her knees, holding Candar by the throat. Then she quickly rose to her feet, tears falling from her eyes. Candar then removed the hand on her throat and rose from the ground.

"You promised me you would protect my husband! You broke your promise!"

"No. I never promised your husband would survive every mission. There are no guarantees in life. There is always risk."

Aurora hit Candar in the chest several times, then pulled away from her and leaned against the door to the house on shaky legs. "What happened?"

"We went to one of Nova Spectrum's bases and stole a fighter. Then we went to a moon base in the Bormino system. We were on a mission for the Grand Oracle. I was to steal data disks while your husband was to stay on board and pilot the ship. We had complications, and when I arrived back on the ship I found him dying."

"You didn't have the decency to bring his body to me and my children?! Where is his body?"

"My ship was damaged and it crashed into the Bormino Ocean. I couldn't retrieve the body."

"Couldn't, or didn't care enough to preserve his body? You are always thinking about yourself while those around you die all the time."

"He was a brave man."

"Those are hollow words that mean nothing to me now."

"I made a promise to Asterism that I would provide for you and your children." Candar threw several bags of gold coins on the ground at Aurora's feet.

Aurora opened the door to her house and came back with a blaster rifle in her hands. "I don't want any of your blood money! Pick it up! Pick it up now and leave!"

Candar picked up the bags of gold coins and placed them back in a pouch around her waist.

"Leave now and if you ever come back here, I will kill you myself or tell Nova Spectrum where to find you."

"Aurora, if you do, you will dishonor your husband, all he stood for, and his memory."

"I should kill you right now!"

"Killing me won't ease your grief."

Aurora raised the blaster rifle and looked like she was about to shoot Candar when she felt a tugging on her dress.

"Mama, don't kill her. It is wrong."

"Get into the house now!"

Candar turned to walk away as the boy entered the house. It was a few minutes later that Candar felt a tugging on her left leg. She turned around and saw the young boy.

"Did my mama hurt you?"

"No, she didn't. She is just in grief. What's your name?"

"It is Pollux."

"Can you keep a secret, Pollux?"

"Yes, I can."

"Good. Now the secret is your dad wanted me to give your mom money. This money will help your family for a long time. I will keep my promise to him. Do you know the Crux Cave?"

"Yes, I've been there."

"Good. Now I will place money in the cave and I want you to find it and bring it to your mother. Don't tell her it is coming from me. Just tell her you found it in the cave."

"Okay, I will do it."

"This money will help you survive. So starting tomorrow, come to the cave and take money back to your mother. Then at the beginning of each week, come to the cave to take more money home."

Candar knelt down and hugged Pollux. "You're a brave boy just like your daddy was. Now go back home so your mother doesn't worry about you."

Pollux turned and started to walk back home while Candar headed for the cave. Once in the cave, she emptied all the bags of gold coins and left. As she walked to where the Aquila was waiting for her, she decided she would have to have some locals she trusted to bring gold coins and place them in the cave once a week to keep her promise to her dear friend Captain Asterism.

Once she made it back to her ship, she plotted a course, wondering if there was some truth to what

Aurora had said. Was she to blame for Asterism's death?

Then another thought entered her mind. No, she wasn't responsible for his death. It was evil that killed him. All she could do now was to stop Nova Spectrum any way she could. She knew she couldn't do this alone. The job was too big for her to handle. She needed someone's help.

Candar left the cockpit of her ship and walked to her quarters, where she fell onto the bed. The autopilot on the ship activated and left the planet, then entered into a hyperspace jump.

"Where are you, Orion Nebula? I need you now," Candar said, her mind blank to where Orion might be at the moment. It was her last thought before she fell asleep.

The Andromeda Force

David Kantorski

Nanithedog.com

677 Lebanon Hill Rd

Southbridge, MA 01550

www.ingramcontent.com/pod-product-compliance
Lightning Source LLC
Chambersburg PA
CBHW061429030726
47503CB00005B/1354